HOT MESS

Hostile Operations Team ® - Book 2

LYNN RAYE HARRIS

All Rights Reserved. This book or any portion thereof
may not be reproduced or used in any manner whatsoever
without the express written permission of the publisher
except for the use of brief quotations in a book review.

This is a work of fiction. Names, characters, places, and incidents either are the products of the author's imagination or are used fictitiously. Any resemblance to actual persons, living or dead, businesses, companies, events, or locales is entirely coincidental.

The Hostile Operations Team® and Lynn Raye Harris® are trademarks of H.O.T. Publishing, LLC.

Printed in the United States of America

First Printing, 2020

For rights inquires, visit www.LynnRayeHarris.com

HOT Mess
HOT MESS - 2019 Expanded Version
Copyright © 2013 by Lynn Raye Harris
Cover Design Copyright © 2013 Croco Designs

ISBN: 978-1-941002-54-4

To my readers! Y'all rock! Thanks for embracing the men of HOT and the women who tame them.

Prologue

Hopeful, Texas

TEXAS SUMMERS MELTED ALL the good sense a man possessed. That was the only explanation for why Sam McKnight had taken Georgeanne Hayes and driven up toward Hopeful Lake. He hadn't intended to do it at all, but since he'd gotten back home on leave from the Army three days ago, he'd noticed one thing in this town that had changed dramatically: Georgie Hayes.

"You home for long?" Georgie asked.

He turned the car—an old truck he'd borrowed from his mother—onto the dirt track that ran around the south side of the lake. It was nearly dark now, the sun a glimmer of a memory on the horizon.

"Just a few days."

"I've missed you, Sam."

He shot her a grin. "I missed you too. Your whole family," he added. The Hayes family had always been more of a family to him than his own. Her brother was his best friend in the world—which meant he should *not* be thinking of Georgie as anything more than the annoying little kid she'd always been. She used to follow him around whenever he was at her house, her barely concealed crush almost embarrassing to witness. He'd ignored it, which hadn't been difficult to do when she'd been twelve and he fifteen.

But now she was eighteen—and impossible to ignore.

He could feel her pouting in the silence that followed. God, she'd changed. In ways he still couldn't wrap his head around.

"I was hoping maybe you'd missed me the most," she said softly.

"If I'd known you'd turn out like this, I might have." *Shut up, Sam.*

Because he knew, as sure as he knew his own name, that he was *not* what Richard Hayes Sr. had in mind for his little princess. Georgie was going to the University of Texas where she'd study something suitably refined—interior design, perhaps—and marry the star quarterback.

He was just a soldier home on leave—and he had nothing to offer besides a healthy libido and a few stolen nights of passion.

"It was inevitable. Mama was Miss Dallas, you know."

Yeah, he knew. But that didn't mean he'd ever thought of Georgie as anything more than Rick's little sister. Yet here she was with curves in all the right places, an impressive rack, and the most gorgeous chocolate-brown hair that tumbled in waves over her shoulders and fell all the way to her ass.

He found a place to park and turned off the engine. His heart pounded in his chest as he turned to look at her. What the hell was he doing again? He needed to drive straight back to town and forget every dirty thought he'd been thinking about her since she'd walked into the bowling alley an hour ago.

She gazed at him with eyes that he felt like he could drown in. Green eyes, like springtime in the country.

"I'm eighteen now."

"I know."

She slicked her tongue over pretty pink lips. "Then maybe you'll finally kiss me."

He could only stare at her for a long moment, his brain warring with his dick. She was still his best friend's baby sister, and he had a duty to protect her just the same as Rick would if he were here. Sam had driven her out here, but only because she'd asked him to.

Dumbass. You know exactly why she asked, and you also know why you did it.

"I'm not sure it's a good idea, Georgie."

She unclipped her seatbelt and moved toward him. "I am. I want to kiss you, Sam. Hell, I want you. I've wanted you since I was thirteen."

He swallowed hard. His voice, when he spoke, was hoarse. "You don't mean that."

She slid up close and put her arms around his neck. "Like hell I don't. Oh, I didn't know what I wanted at thirteen. But I do now. I want *you*, Sam. I want you to fuck me."

"Christ, Georgie, don't talk like that." His hands spanned her ribcage. He intended to set her away from him, but somehow he wasn't managing it.

And Georgie knew it.

"Why not? Does it turn you on?"

Did it turn him on? Shit, he was harder than an ice cube in Siberia. "I'm not here to stay. You know that, right? I gotta leave in two days and go back to the Army."

"I know."

"You asked me if I was home for long."

She sighed. "Small talk, Sam. I know you aren't staying. But I want you anyway."

He shouldn't do it. He knew he shouldn't. He should start the truck and drive back toward town. But he wasn't going to. He was weak and, from the moment she'd walked up to him looking like this, he was lost.

With a groan, Sam lowered his mouth to hers and kissed her.

Chapter One

TWELVE YEARS LATER...

"I'M SORRY, Dr. Hayes, but we can't give out that kind of information."

Georgie gritted her teeth in frustration. She'd been getting the same answer for two days now. Military bureaucracy at its finest. She gripped the phone and tried to keep her voice calm. "Sergeant Hamilton has not formally withdrawn, but he's not been to class for the last three sessions. Surely you know if he's been deployed."

The woman on the other end didn't miss a beat. "I'm not allowed to give out that information, Dr. Hayes. We don't discuss our personnel with unauthorized persons."

Georgie sighed and pressed her hand to her forehead. "Fine. Can someone just submit a withdrawal form on his behalf? It will save him getting an F, which will affect his GPA."

And if she knew anything about Jake Hamilton, she knew for a fact he didn't want that. He was dead set on graduating with honors and applying for Officer Training School. If it came down to it, she'd submit the form herself. It was against policy, but she'd argue for an exception in this case.

"I'll see what we can do."

After the niceties were finished, Georgie hung up the phone and suppressed the urge to scream. If she were at home alone, in her little Alexandria townhouse, she might do just that. But she was currently sitting in a coffee shop in the Pentagon concourse, waiting for her class to start.

The military did a fine job of encouraging its members to go to school, gave them plenty of money for tuition, and provided space on military installations around the world for universities to teach classes and offer degree programs. The only issue for most of her students was time since they also had very demanding jobs.

Which was where her concern for Sergeant Hamilton had come in. This was the third course he'd taken with her, and she'd never known him to miss a single session without first informing her of any temporary duty he might have. Not that he couldn't have had an emergency, but when he missed the third class in a row, she'd begun to wonder. It just wasn't like him to be irresponsible.

If he didn't show up tonight, it would be the fourth

time. Two weeks of class was a lot in an eight-week term. Not only that, but finals were next week, and if he didn't come tonight, he'd never be prepared. She'd e-mailed him a couple of times now, and she'd even called the number he'd put on the information sheet she collected from every student at the beginning of the term.

There had been no reply to her calls or her e-mails, which seemed very odd.

The last time she'd seen Jake, he'd been sitting on a bench in the Pentagon Metro. She'd walked over to talk to him before the train arrived. He'd seemed a bit preoccupied, but she hadn't thought too much about it since her students were adults with busy lives.

When the train came, he did not get on. He'd told her he was waiting for a friend so they could go out to a bar in Crystal City. The last Georgie had seen of him, he'd been talking to a dark-haired man with a manicured beard. Georgie had waved again as the train pulled out. The man standing with Jake turned, his hard gaze meeting hers. He'd looked angry, threatening in a way that shocked her. She'd snatched her hand into her lap and turned her head, breaking eye contact.

And then she'd been angry with herself for reacting that way. She was a grown woman, independent, and she didn't like that a man had made her feel unsafe just by looking at her angrily.

But then she'd gone home, taken a hot bath, immersed herself in a book, and forgotten about Jake and his friend.

Now Georgie checked the time on her phone, and

then she gathered her computer and purse and made her way down to the basement where her class was being held.

Jake never showed. Two and a half hours later she retraced her path through the Pentagon and down to the Metro station that lay beneath the building.

As she stood in the station with the hot air blowing through the tunnels and ruffling her hair, she decided that tomorrow she was calling that woman at Jake Hamilton's unit and trying again.

She knew she should just leave well enough alone, knew that the military did what they wanted when they wanted. They could have shipped him off in the middle of the night for some sort of duty, but he wasn't Special Forces. He worked in a general's office as an administrative assistant. Not typically the kind of guy to disappear without notice since he wasn't a combat troop.

Georgie yawned and stepped forward as the rush of air intensified ahead of the next train. She was so ready to take a hot bath and climb into bed with a good book and her cat. The sad state of her life these days. Being divorced was a blessing, but it certainly hadn't done anything for her social life.

A bright light shone from the tunnel as the train fast approached. The station wasn't as crowded this time of night as it was during rush hour, but there were still plenty of people waiting on the platform. Georgie was moving toward the platform's edge along with everyone else when someone jostled her. Hard.

She lost her balance and slammed onto the concrete,

her body sliding over the lip before she could save herself.

The darkness below yawned up at her as the train's brakes began to screech. Her body seemed to hang over inky blackness for a long moment, her arms useless to grab onto anything because there was nothing to grab.

And then she was falling, falling, falling—into the path of the train.

Georgie screamed.

Chapter Two

STAFF SERGEANT SAM MCKNIGHT STOOD IN FRONT OF A townhouse on a shaded Alexandria street and took a deep breath. It was early morning and the sun was shining bright. The sky already had that hazy look that meant they were in for another humid day in the DC Metro area. It was hotter than blazes, but not quite as hot as Texas. Or as hot as where he'd just returned from.

Texas might be hot, but the Afghan desert was hotter. He could say that for a fact now that he'd been on rotation there with his Ranger unit. He expected he'd get there a few more times now that he'd joined the Hostile Operations Team.

He looked down at his uniform—crisp ACUs—and wondered if he should have saved this visit for another time, when he could show up in jeans and a T-shirt and look halfway like the guy Georgie would remember.

But he'd just gotten back to the States recently and he was looking forward to seeing an old friend—at least he hoped Georgie was still his friend. He hadn't known she was in DC until he'd spoken to Rick just a few days ago.

"Could you check on her for me, man?" Rick had asked. "I think the divorce messed with her head. She seems sad. Won't come home to Texas, insists on staying in DC and teaching college classes."

Sam frowned. He had no idea what kind of reception Georgie might give him. He hadn't seen her since she'd married Tim Cash six years ago. Before that, the last time he'd seen her was when she'd been naked in the front seat of his truck and he'd nearly taken everything she'd offered. He'd had the good sense to stop, but he wasn't sure she'd ever forgiven him for it.

"I don't know if that's a good idea, Rick. Why don't you just call her and ask how she is?"

Rick blew out a breath. "I call her every week, but she never says anything. She avoids my questions about Tim and says she's fine. I'll send you her address. Just go see her. She'll be thrilled."

Sam fixed his gaze on her door. Birds chirped in the trees overhead as he steeled his backbone and prepared to ring the bell. Hell, he wanted to see Georgie. He just wasn't certain she wanted to see him.

When he'd heard she was marrying that dick Timothy Cash, he swore he wouldn't go to the wedding. But then the invitation had arrived, and though he'd replied no, he'd flown home at the last minute and walked into the reception, compelled by some force he hadn't quite understood.

He had never forgotten the sight of Georgie in her

wedding dress, or the way it had somehow managed to jab him right in the chest and make him ache for days. He hadn't seen her since that day six years ago. Was he ready to see her now?

Sam took a deep breath and stepped up to the door. He was *not* scared of a little girl from his hometown just because she twisted him up inside.

No fucking way.

Sam jabbed the doorbell and waited. No one came. He jabbed the bell again and stepped back to look up at the house. A curtain moved in a window above. He didn't know if that meant she would come to the door or not, but he wasn't going away now that he knew she was home. Georgie couldn't ignore him forever.

It took almost five minutes, but he heard movement inside. And then the door whipped open and Georgie was standing there, staring at him with the most God-awful, wounded-looking eyes. Jesus, had he put that look on her face? Or had Tim really hurt her that badly?

Sam wanted to drag her into his arms and hold her tight. "Hello, Georgie."

She blinked. And then a slow smile appeared. It wasn't a bright smile, but it was a smile nonetheless. "Hey, Sam." Her gaze slid over him. "Long time, no see. Get lost on your way to work?"

"Naw." He stood there looking at her, just drinking her in and feeling that same jab in the chest he'd felt six years ago. Why? That's what he didn't get. She was just little Georgie Hayes, his best friend's pain-in-the-ass baby sister.

She stood there in a stretchy tank top and what he'd

been told were yoga pants, her body lush with those curves that had nearly done him in twelve years ago. Her green eyes were deep and mysterious, and her brown hair was piled on her head in a messy knot. She looked adorably rumpled, and he had a sudden thought that maybe she wasn't precisely alone.

Which jabbed him in the chest a little bit harder than before.

She held the door open wide. "Do you want to come in?"

"That would be great."

She stepped back and he entered, shutting the door behind him. Her foyer was dark and cool and he stood there like an idiot, waiting for her to say something. He figured if he was interrupting something, she might not let him in. On the other hand, he didn't really know what Georgie would do these days.

She turned without speaking and he followed as she walked down the hallway. Sam frowned when he realized she was limping.

"You okay, G?"

Her shoulders stiffened momentarily. "Fine. I fell last night and got a little bruised."

He didn't know why, but that made his hackles rise. She'd been divorced from Tim for months, and while Tim was a class-A prick, Sam had never known him to be violent. But what if Georgie was seeing some guy who was?

Sam would kill him, that's what.

Georgie entered a bright kitchen at the back of the

house and walked over to the counter. "I was just coming down for coffee. You want some?"

"Sure."

Sam stood there with his Army-issue beret in his hands and watched her move. She was stiff, but still so graceful. She grabbed two delicate-looking white cups and saucers from her cabinet.

Georgeanne Hayes was Texas money, debutante balls, exclusive sororities, and country club all the way. She knew which fork to use, what to wear to any event, and she used bone china for her morning coffee.

He was nothing but a poor kid from a broken and dysfunctional family. The Hayeses had looked out for him as much as they were able, but he'd pretty much known from the time he'd been about thirteen that the military was his future. It guaranteed him a way out of Hopeful when nothing else would. Georgie's father had talked to him once about college, about helping him apply for student loans and getting him a job to pay the money back when he was through.

Sam had been too proud to accept that kind of help. And too embarrassed to admit he didn't think he was college material. His daddy grew angry over the time he spent with the Hayeses, accused him of "putting on airs." Well, he wasn't putting on airs, dammit, and he'd forged his own way in life. Maybe he wasn't college educated, but he could damn well do things his father couldn't.

For that matter, he could do things that Rick and Mr. Hayes couldn't either. Not that they needed to know how to breach a steel door, rescue a hostage before the clock ran out, or hit a bull's-eye blindfolded. But he could, and it made him proud.

Georgie fixed the coffee and pushed it at him over the counter. "Cream and sugar?"

"No, thanks." He took the delicate cup and saucer and held them without drinking.

Georgie fixed her own and then looked him in the eye. "Did Rick send you?"

He wasn't surprised at her directness. "Of course he did. But I'm here because I want to be. It's good to see you, Georgie."

She sighed, her shoulders slumping just a little. "I'm sorry, I've just been under some strain lately. I'm glad to see you, Sam. Glad you're looking well. Rick told me you were in Afghanistan and Iraq lately. I was worried about you."

Her concern made a lump form in his throat. "Yeah, I'm fine. Thanks for thinking about me."

She studied him in a way he wasn't quite accustomed to from her. "It's been six years. I didn't think I'd see you again after all this time. I even thought maybe you were avoiding me."

Maybe he had been. A little. "I never doubted we'd see each other eventually. Just been busy—and deployed. A lot."

"You've certainly been gone a long time."

"It's what I signed up for."

She closed her eyes and tilted her head slowly to either side, stretching her muscles. He tried not to focus on the creamy skin of her neck while she moved so sensuously. He'd once had his mouth on that skin.

He'd wanted, so badly, to put his mouth in other places too.

"So what did Rick say? Check up on Georgie because I think she's gone off her rocker?"

Sam snorted a laugh. "Not quite. But yeah, he's worried about you."

She came around the island and headed for the family room. When she settled on the couch, tucking her knees beneath her, Sam didn't miss the way she grimaced. He sank onto a chair opposite.

"I'm doing okay," she said. "Tim and I just grew apart. It wasn't the most pleasant thing I've ever been through, but the divorce was final almost a year ago now. I've moved on."

He searched her face for signs of strain. "Rick thinks you should go home to Texas."

She blinked at him. "And do what? Attend country club gatherings with my mother? Join the Junior League?" She shook her head. "I like DC. And I like what I do so I'm staying. The last I checked, I was all grown up. And that's one of the perks."

Man, no wonder Rick had asked him to talk to her. Georgie wasn't about to be pushed around. Unlike when they'd been kids. He was three years older than her and that made a huge difference at a young age. Now, not so much. "Didn't peg you for a college professor."

She shrugged. "I always wanted to be a writer, so the English degree was no stretch. Turns out I enjoy the teaching more than the writing, so here I am."

"I'm sure you're great at what you do. The college kids must love you."

She laughed. "They aren't really kids, Sam. Didn't Rick tell you?" When he shook his head, she kept going. "I teach in the adult education program. My students are men and women like you. I'm at the Pentagon two nights a week, at Bolling two nights, and Quantico some weekends." She took a sip of her coffee. "Enough about me. Tell me about you. What are you doing in DC?"

He couldn't tell her about HOT. That wasn't authorized. Now that he'd in-processed, he was pulling duty out at their smoking new training facility on a military base in Maryland. Getting to know the guys he'd be working with, the routines, everything. HOT had only moved to DC a few weeks ago. Before that they'd been down at Fort Bragg.

"Just got here for a new assignment. When I called Rick, he told me you were here."

"Tim took a job in DC two years ago. I followed him, of course. Left a good job at the University of Texas, too."

Sam leaned forward. He wanted to touch her, but he wisely refrained. "I'm sorry it didn't work out, Georgie."

She swallowed. And then she shrugged as if it were nothing. "Sometimes it doesn't. Lesson learned and all that."

Sam set the coffee down on the end table. He knew about marriages that didn't work out. He couldn't imagine Tim Cash screaming at Georgie the way his father had screamed at his mother though. Couldn't imagine Georgie crying and begging for another chance. The idea of her crying over that dickhead made him sick.

As if she'd just remembered why he'd spent so much time at her house as a kid, her expression changed into something that looked too much like pity for comfort. "Oh, Sam, I didn't mean—"

He stood abruptly. The one thing he couldn't stomach from anyone was pity. "I have to get to work, Georgie. I just wanted to stop by and see how you were."

She looked up at him, her eyes bright. He hoped those weren't tears. If they were, he was sunk. Georgie Hayes crying always brought out his protective instincts. She bit her lip and looked away again. "Of course. But can I ask you something first?"

A wave of tension rolled through him. He had no idea what the fuck she might ask. But he couldn't refuse her when it seemed such an easy thing on the surface.

"Anything, G. You can ask me anything."

Chapter Three

Georgie couldn't believe that Sam McKnight was standing in her house, looking so damn handsome and perfect and remote that she wanted to scream. When she'd been old enough to notice boys, he'd been everything she'd ever wanted. Three years older than she was, he hadn't been interested in the least. But he'd given her a lot of angsty nights dreaming about him.

He'd spent a lot of time at the Hayeses' house. His parents didn't have much money and they all lived in a run-down trailer in the middle of a field about six miles from town. She remembered one summer when Sam had stayed at their house from the day school let out until right before it started again. Her parents hadn't minded. Rick was happy to have his best friend around and Georgie was happy to gaze blissfully at Sam over the dinner table every night.

She remembered when his parents divorced, too. He'd been sixteen, and he'd grown tight-lipped and sullen. He and Rick spent hours playing their guitars and sneaking Dad's beer from the pool-house fridge. By then she'd been a love-struck thirteen-year-old. She'd spent hours writing *Mrs. Georgeanne McKnight* in her diary. And she'd followed him around, asking questions, trying to get him to notice her.

He had, but never as anything more than Rick's annoying little sister. He'd treated her exactly as Rick had treated her. Except for that one extremely memorable time when she'd been eighteen. Holy smokes, what a night that had almost been. She could still taste the disappointment and humiliation of being pushed away as if it were yesterday.

She'd been burning up for him, wet and ready—and he'd stopped right before he'd gotten to the good part. Her fault. Shame still burned inside her when she thought of it. She only hoped it didn't show on her face.

Right now she'd blundered when she'd started talking about divorce and relationships not working out. Sometimes it wasn't so simple. Sometimes people grew to hate each other, and sometimes they dragged their kids into the hell they created. Sam had been torn between parents who viciously despised each other and who used him as a weapon in their war. He'd suffered. She'd known it on some level, even as a thirteen-year-old.

Georgie swallowed the lump in her throat. She was on edge, emotional, and a big part of it was due to seeing him again. Six years, and he still had the ability to make her heart speed up.

My God.

He'd always been handsome, but now? Now he was

big and full of hard muscle that shifted beneath his shirt when he moved. His hair was short, though not as short as she was used to seeing on many of her Army students. His eyes were the most remarkable thing, though. They had depths she didn't remember. Hidden secrets.

"I… I was just wondering if you knew how I could find out if a soldier has been deployed. I've tried his unit orderly room, but they won't tell me."

Sam's brows drew down and she knew he was thinking not only about what she'd asked him, but also about why she wanted to know. She didn't know why she'd tossed it out there, except that Sam was in the Army and maybe he knew how these things worked. Clearly, she didn't.

"Why do you need to know if someone has been deployed?"

She shifted on the couch, her aching muscles protesting the movement. She'd nearly taken a dive onto the tracks last night, but just as she felt herself falling into the darkness below the platform, a man had grabbed her and pulled her free. She hadn't seen his face, but she was forever grateful to him.

Sam was still gazing at her with a look of bafflement—and maybe concern—on his face.

"I have a student who stopped coming to class. It's unusual."

Sam frowned for a second. And then he shook his head. She wondered if he'd been expecting her to say something else.

"Not for an active-duty soldier. Things come up, sometimes at a moment's notice."

She could feel fresh heat creeping into her cheeks. Hadn't she thought the same thing herself? "He worked in General Porter's office."

Sam eyes narrowed. "Porter's part of DARPA. Maybe the guy had to go somewhere for a test."

She'd been working with the military for over a year now and the acronyms still went over her head sometimes. "DARPA? What's that?"

"It's the Defense Advanced Research Projects Agency. They work on technological projects designed to advance military capabilities around the globe. Real cloak-and-dagger stuff."

Georgie shivered. Jake worked on cloak-and-dagger projects? "Sounds very secretive."

"It is. But what I just told you is the kind of thing you'd find on Wikipedia. The projects are classified, but not the existence of the agency or their basic mission."

Georgie frowned as she studied the coffee in her hands. She was being silly. Jake had been sent somewhere and it was far more important to him than the possibility of a less-than-perfect GPA. "So he could have just gone away at a moment's notice?"

"Very possible."

Yet she couldn't forget that night in the Metro when he'd been talking to the man who'd given her a vaguely uneasy feeling. "I guess I can't verify it in any way."

"Probably not." After a moment, Sam sighed, his rigid stance relaxing a hair. "Give me his name and I'll see what I can find out. I'm not promising anything, but maybe if I ask the right people I can find out when he'll be back."

"That would be amazing. Army Sergeant Jake Hamilton."

Sam slapped the beret against his leg. "I really have to go, G. I have to get out to Maryland before the traffic gets too bad."

Georgie dragged herself up, wincing as she put weight on her leg. "I appreciate you checking into this for me."

Sam's expression had turned hard, as if he wanted to punch something. It disconcerted her for a moment, but then she realized it was just his protective instincts coming out at the evidence of her discomfort. No bully had ever bothered her for long with Sam and Rick around.

"You need to take a hot bath and relax."

She smiled. "Did that last night. I imagine the bruising will only get worse before it gets better."

Sam shoved a hand through his hair, which was sort of senseless since it was cropped so short. It was completely sexy on him. As were the muscles. Georgie forced herself to concentrate on his dark, glittering eyes. *Put those muscles from your mind, girl.*

"How did you fall?"

"Someone bumped into me in the Metro. I went down hard."

It was the truth, though she left out the part about nearly falling into a train's path. Sam wouldn't hesitate to call Rick about it, and then Rick would call their mother. Cynthia Tolliver Hayes would be on the next plane to DC. Georgie suppressed a shudder. She loved her mother but the woman would suffocate her if she showed up.

Sam took a card from his pocket and wrote a number on it with the pen sitting on her coffee table. His tanned fingers were long and strong, and she found herself shivering involuntarily as she watched him write. Then he straightened again and she tried to force her mind away from his hands.

Hands that had once caressed her so sweetly she'd nearly cried. He'd slid a finger into her wet folds, stroked her until she'd sobbed his name. Her body clenched with the memory, even now. It had been far too long since she'd desired a man, far too long since she'd felt anything remotely like need flare deep inside her.

But right now if Sam McKnight asked her to strip naked and lie back on the sofa, she'd do it in a heartbeat.

"Call me if you need anything, Georgie."

She tried not to swallow her tongue. *If she needed anything*.

Gawd almighty.

She took the card, and then they stood there awkwardly for several moments while she wondered whether she should give him a friendly hug. How did you hug a man you'd once wanted with every ounce of desire in your body? A man who was currently making you zing with sparks you hadn't felt in a long damn time?

"Goodbye, Georgie."

Her heart turned over but she managed to smile. "Bye, Sam. It was great seeing you."

"You too." He hesitated so long she thought he might say something else, but then he turned and walked back down the hallway. She listened to the door snick closed behind him, and then she cursed herself up one side and down the other.

Way to go, Georgie-girl.

Chapter Four

Sam prowled around HOT headquarters like an angry lion. He didn't know why he was so worked up over Georgie needing to know about a soldier. But he was. He could still hear the way she said the guy's name, with such concern, until it twisted up inside his brain and made him want to dig it out by any means possible.

Jake Hamilton. She'd said he was just a good student she was concerned about, but she sounded almost fond of the guy. What if there was more to it than that? What if she had a thing going with Jake Hamilton and didn't want to admit it?

The thought didn't sit quite right with Sam, though God knew he didn't have even the ghost of a reason to be upset about it. He'd given up that right a long time ago.

Georgie was off-limits to him. Always had been, even if he'd nearly fucked it up once.

He could still taste her sweet mouth, the nectar of her pussy on his fingers, the drumbeat of hot desire that had pounded in his brain until he'd been nearly mindless with the urge to slide into her body and give them both some sweet relief.

But then she'd whispered that she was still a virgin—that she'd saved herself for him—and he'd known he had to stop. How could he take what she offered with a clear conscience, knowing he could never give her more than a few stolen nights? Georgie had convinced herself she was in love with him when all he wanted was sex. If she'd been anybody else, he might not have cared. But she was Georgie, and he knew he couldn't break her heart like that.

Aside from that one incident, she was like a sister to him. He'd spent long summers at her house, pretending not to notice her following him around like a lovesick puppy, and he'd grown to care about her. Hell, he cared about all the Hayeses. Rick, his mom and dad, and little Georgie. They'd given him shelter when he'd had none, given him a place to be a kid when his house was nothing but a battleground.

That was why he'd do whatever he could for any of them. So if Georgie was concerned about Sergeant Hamilton, then Sam would do his best. And he wouldn't feel a pinch in his heart over the way she said the guy's name or the blatant concern on her face or the thought there might be more between her and this soldier than she'd admitted.

Sam walked back inside the offices where his new team was located and plopped down at the desk he'd been assigned. There was nothing on it yet but a computer and some binders containing mission briefs.

He was pumped to be here, but he couldn't give it his full concentration just yet.

"Yo, Knight Rider, you got everything you need?"

Sam looked up to find Kevin MacDonald standing over him. Big Mac was the second-in-command of their team. No one else was around right now except Billy "the Kid" Blake, who sat hunched over his computer, fingers flying as he worked to crack some kind of code or write a program. Or, hell, maybe he was hacking into China or something.

Sam had no idea since that wasn't his thing. Weapons, that was his deal. Just give him some guns or explosives and he was good to go. The other new guy, Garrett "Iceman" Spencer, was much the same. They'd already talked about their favorite types of breaching devices and compared notes.

Sam threw a glance at Kid. It had definitely crossed his mind that Kid could find Jake Hamilton. If Sam could ever manage to ask about it. Sam was still new enough that he wasn't quite sure about these guys yet. He'd been training with them pretty hard, and he knew they were all brilliant at what they did. He had no doubt his ass would be safer than all the gold in Fort Knox when he was out on a mission with HOT. But that didn't mean he felt comfortable enough to ask for information he wanted for personal reasons.

"Yeah, man. Doing great," he answered.

Big Mac sank into a chair opposite. "So, you go see your friend?"

"Before work." He tapped his fingers on the desk. If he didn't at least float the idea, he'd never know. Maybe he'd get an answer. Maybe he wouldn't. But at least he'd know the boundaries then. "She teaches college classes at the Pentagon. Says one of her students is missing. An active-duty guy."

Big Mac frowned. "Probably a short-notice deployment."

"That's what I told her. She isn't convinced, and no one will give her any information." He leaned back in the seat, bouncing it a little bit. "The guy works for DARPA. Nothing unusual in a short-notice assignment."

Big Mac shrugged. "Ask Kid. He could locate the record in half a minute. If it's classified, that's the end of it. But maybe he had emergency leave or something. At least then you could tell her not to worry." He grinned. "Or maybe you want the guy to stay gone? Give you a chance, right? Is she pretty?"

Sam couldn't find his voice. Was she pretty? Hell, yeah. Pretty—and so fucking sexy he could grow hard thinking about her. But he wouldn't. He had too much self-discipline for that.

Riiiight.

He cleared his throat. "She's like a sister to me, dude. I grew up with her and her brother."

"Ah." Big Mac stood. "Well then, different story. Hey, Kid, got something for you," he called. Then he winked at Sam and strode out of the room.

Sam glanced over at Billy Blake, who was looking at him quizzically. "What d'you need, man?"

GEORGIE DECIDED she needed to get out of the house. She had no classes today, but that still wasn't an excuse to lie around and do nothing. Besides, sitting at home, all she could seem to think about was Sam standing in her living room and the mixed-up tangle of emotions she'd felt from the moment she opened the door and saw him on her threshold.

It was early on an August day, and the humidity was already approaching unbearable. Still, Georgie forged onward until she reached her favorite café, ordered a latte, and took a seat in the corner where she could watch people go by. She'd been there for about a half hour, scrolling through e-mail on her laptop, when a man sat down across from her.

She looked up in surprise. The café wasn't full and there were plenty of other tables.

"Hi," he said, smiling. He was dark eyed, dark skinned, quite possible Middle Eastern though she didn't know for sure. His smile did not reach his eyes.

"Can I help you?" She infused her voice with her best frosty tone, learned at the feet of her debutante mother, and waited for him to take the hint.

"You're pretty," he said.

"Thank you, but I'm not interested."

He reached for her hand, gripping it in a surprisingly strong hold. Georgie tried to jerk away but he held her tight. Her heart hammered and her stomach bottomed out as a wave of bitter acid flooded her tongue. She opened her mouth to yell for help.

Before she could say anything, the man leaned forward, his eyes gleaming with malice. "Your boyfriend lied to us, Dr. Hayes. If you don't wish to fall onto the tracks the next time, you will give us the information he promised. We will be in touch."

He let her go and shoved back from the table. Georgie sat there with her heart in her throat, her skin flushing hot. Her boyfriend? What the hell? She wanted to call out and tell him he had the wrong person, in spite of the fact he'd used her name, but the man was gone.

A river of ice poured down her spine as the rest of his words sank in.

Last night hadn't been an accident. Someone had actually pushed her on purpose. Had they saved her too?

Bile rolled in sickening waves in her belly.

Georgie sucked in a breath, and then another and another as she tried not to hyperventilate. Cold fear gripped her hard, shaking her until her entire body trembled uncontrollably. She darted her gaze around the coffee shop but no one seemed to be interested in her. Hastily, she grabbed her things and shoved them into her bag with hands that shook so hard she could barely perform the task.

The day was bright, the streets filled with tourists and residents alike. She told herself no one would approach her again as she hurried home. She wanted to be inside her house where no stranger could grab her like he had the right. Where no one could threaten her.

She reached her street, flew up her steps, and put her key into the lock with trembling fingers. Once inside, she locked the door behind her and let out a shaky sigh. She set her purse on the table in the hall and headed toward the kitchen. A glass of ice with some vodka and tonic—heavy on the vodka—was just what she needed. Then she could think again.

Maybe she'd call Sam and tell him about it, get his advice. Or maybe she wouldn't because Sam would probably tell Rick.

Fear clutched her heart in a cold fist as she stepped into the kitchen.

The back door stood wide open.

Chapter Five

GEORGIE WAS NOT ONE TO FALL APART. SHE'D BEEN raised to be gracious, strong, and flexible in all things. Her mother was pure Texas steel and her father had more grit than a beach. But this was not the same as dealing with a surly waiter or a pushy car salesman. This was dead serious and far outside her area of expertise.

The instant she saw the open door she sprinted back through the house and out the front, snagging her purse along the way. There were people on the street, tourists walking through Old Town, and she was reasonably certain nobody would try to grab her in front of witnesses. Shivering, she whipped out her cell phone and called the first person she could think of.

Sam answered on the third ring. Relief made her knees wobble. His voice was warm and gravelly and she wanted to wrap it around her like a blanket.

"Hi, Georgie."

Tears pressed against the backs of her eyes. "Sam," she said hoarsely.

"Georgie? What's wrong?"

She loved that he instantly knew. He sounded intense, determined. Protective.

"I—I think someone was in my house."

"In your house? Are you there now?"

"N-no. I'm outside." She dragged in air. "I-I went to the coffee shop on the corner. There was a man. He sat at my table and grabbed my hand and wouldn't let go. Then he said th-that my boyfriend lied to him and he wanted the information. He said he'd be in touch. I don't know what information he's talking about—and I don't have a boyfriend either. When I got home, the back door was open—I panicked."

Sam's voice was strong and hard-edged as a diamond. "Is there a neighbor's house you can go to?"

"Yes. My next-door neighbor. She's a stay-at-home mom with toddlers. She's usually there."

"Go. I'll stay on the phone until she answers the door."

"Okay." Her throat was tight. "My cat—I didn't look for her. She's inside—" Her voice choked off.

Belle was the kind of cat who hid whenever she heard a noise, so she had to be okay. She *had* to. She'd be tucked under the bed or the couch—and even if she came out, she wouldn't leave the relative safety of the house.

"I'll be there as soon as I can. Don't worry, Georgie. We'll find her. And I won't let anything happen to either of you."

She believed him. "Hurry, Sam. Please hurry."

"I'm on my way. Now get inside so I can stop worrying about you exposed on the street."

Georgie dashed up her neighbor's steps and rang the bell. Sam hung up once Sissy let her in. Sissy sat her down and went to fix a pot of tea.

Georgie pulled in a breath and tried to think logically. Maybe she should have called the police instead of Sam, but he'd been the first person she'd thought of.

If he thought she needed to call the police after he checked everything out, then she would. If she was wrong about somebody being inside and it was her own carelessness at fault, she didn't need to waste police time.

Sissy brought a tray with hot tea, her pretty face bordering on terrified. "I've been telling Don we need to install an alarm system." She picked up her cup, her fingers trembling. In the background, her toddlers screamed along to something on the television. "What if someone tried to break in here when it's just me and the girls?"

Georgie willed her thumping heart to beat a little slower. "I'm sure I must have left the door unlocked," she said, wanting to calm Sissy's fears as much as her own. "Someone could have just walked right in. Or maybe I didn't push it all the way closed and it worked itself free while I was gone."

Sissy chewed her lip. "That's possible. And it's not like we've had a rash of break-ins. Still, I'll feel better once we get that alarm. Maybe we should call the police, just in case…"

"I already called my friend. He's a badass military guy, so I know he'll make sure everything is fine. If he thinks someone broke in and I should call the police, I will."

Sissy nodded. "That sounds sensible. It's not like the police don't have enough to do, right?"

"Right."

But there was a downside to calling Sam, and Georgie had been thinking about that too—not that she'd thought of it when she'd first dialed. But what if he told Rick? *Oh mercy...*

She'd never hear the end of it. Her brother would very likely hop on a plane and come here to try and force her back to Texas. Which would result in a fight of epic proportions. She hadn't tucked her tail and ran when her life with Tim fell apart. She wasn't running now.

The phone chose that moment to blare and Georgie jumped in spite of the noise of the television and Sissy's toddlers. Sissy snatched it up and started filling her husband in.

Georgie clutched her cup in her fingers and went over everything in her mind from the moment she'd left the house until she returned. Had she left the door unlocked? Could it have swung open from the pressure when she'd closed the front door? It had happened before, when she'd first moved in, but not for a long time now.

Georgie wanted to go back and check for Belle, but she knew better. All she could do was wait for Sam to arrive while second-guessing herself every possible way.

Within the hour, someone banged on the door. Georgie and Sissy both jumped, but then Sissy got up and went to answer it. A moment later Sam entered the room and a wave of relief washed over Georgie. She didn't even hesitate before getting up and flinging herself into his arms. It was as natural as breathing.

He seemed stunned at first, but then his arms tightened around her. "You're okay," he said softly. "And Belle is okay too. There's no one there."

She sucked in a shaky breath and pushed back to look up at him. He was blurry.

"You're sure? She's really okay?" Logically, she knew her kitty was fine. Belle didn't trust easily.

"Yes, she's okay. She was hiding beneath the couch." His dark eyes gleamed hot, and she knew he was suppressing something. She'd always known when Sam was shoving his feelings deep and twisting the screws down on the lid. It made her heart throb and her stomach clench tight.

"I want to see her."

"Sure."

Georgie didn't ask if he'd discovered whether or not someone had broken in because she didn't want to alarm Sissy. There was time for that when they were alone.

She thanked Sissy, and then she and Sam went next door and into her house, which he'd locked up tight before coming over to get her. She stooped down and called for Belle, who came trotting and meowing almost immediately. Georgie picked her up and stroked her soft fur. Belle purred as if nothing out of the ordinary had happened.

"Could you tell if anyone was in here?" she asked Sam.

"The lock on the back door was forced."

Georgie's belly twisted. "Is that all?"

"No. Come on and I'll show you."

Georgie buried her nose in Belle's caramel fur and rubbed her cheek against the cat's soft body as she followed Sam to the kitchen. Belle continued to purr happily.

Thank God.

As soon as they walked in, Georgie noticed what she hadn't noticed before. She'd vaguely thought something was out of place, but the second she'd seen the open door, she hadn't stayed to look around.

The papers and books on her kitchen table were dumped on the floor. Drawers were torn open in the credenza that sat in the eat-in part of the kitchen.

Her gaze met Sam's. He looked quietly furious. "Is there more?"

"Somebody went through your drawers in your office, and upstairs in your room. They got about halfway through your closet before you returned. You must have scared them."

Georgie felt her color drain away. "You mean somebody was inside when I came back?"

"Probably."

"I should call the police. Shouldn't I?"

"Why don't you see if anything's missing first." It wasn't a question.

Georgie put Belle down and nodded. "I hadn't thought of that. I mean if it was a robbery, why didn't they take that silver serving bowl on the table? Or the desktop computer in my office? Or my television?"

She had a lot of stuff that a thief should have taken, but everywhere she looked, nothing was missing. She went up to her bedroom, Sam on her heels. Her drawers were ransacked and her closet was tossed about, but it was all there.

Sam was frowning, hands in pockets as he watched her. "Based on what you told me about the coffee shop, I think the two events are connected. Which means these guys weren't looking to steal from you. You can call the police if you want, but they aren't going to find who did this."

Georgie blinked at her surroundings. This was her bedroom, the place where she slept at night. Her retreat. And someone had been in here, pawing through her stuff.

"I don't want to stay here tonight."

"I wasn't planning to let you. Pack your things and let's get out of here."

Georgie's heart twisted. She wanted to do exactly as he said and give away the responsibility for this situation, yet she'd learned a hard lesson with Tim. Never give your power to a man. Never let a man control you.

Should she go with Sam, or should she check into a hotel for the night? If she checked into a hotel, then she'd still be making her own decisions.

"But then what? Who's going to find them?" Georgie shook her head, confused. "Maybe I should just stay, face the fear. I have a shotgun. I could sleep with it by the bed. And if they didn't find what they were looking for, maybe they won't come back. Maybe this was the end of it."

Sam stepped forward, and she realized again just how big and hard he was. In spite of herself, a little flame leapt and curled in her belly.

Sam McKnight. Still so handsome. Still so remote.

And still not interested in Georgie Hayes.

Not that she needed to be worrying about that right now, but it was somehow easier to concentrate on Sam and all her latent feelings than on the fact someone had threatened her just an hour ago.

"I wasn't giving you a choice. Get packed."

Something in his tone rubbed her the wrong way, making her think of days long ago. "I'm not twelve anymore, and you can't tell me what to do. I have a life, a job. And my cat. I can't just leave her."

"Take her with you. But you *are* leaving, Georgie. One way or the other."

"What's that supposed to mean?"

His eyes glittered with determination. "It means I'll throw you over my shoulder if I have to."

Georgie swallowed. "How do I know you aren't just being overprotective because you think you owe Rick something?"

She knew it was more than that, but old habits died hard. Rick and Sam had always been there, ready to beat up anyone and everyone who looked at her cross-eyed. This was so much more than childhood bullies, though. They both knew it.

Sam swore, soft and low. "All right. I wasn't going to

tell you this just yet, but you need to come with me because I found Jake Hamilton for you—"

"You found Jake?" Oh my God, she'd nearly forgotten about Jake over the last couple of hours. How had that happened?

He nodded, his expression firm and unhappy at the same time. Dread took up residence in her heart.

"He's not coming back, Georgie."

"Something happened to him?" Her voice was little more than a whisper. She'd known it. Somehow, she'd known.

Sam nodded. "Yes."

Her legs just sort of collapsed beneath her. She found herself sitting on her bed, looking up at Sam through a haze of tears. "I don't understand."

Sam came over and hunkered down in front of her. He brushed the tears off her cheeks. "I need you to trust me, Georgie. I need you to pack some things, get your cat, and come with me. This is a lot bigger than you realize. And a lot more dangerous."

She sucked in another breath and tried not to lose it. "I have no idea what's going on. Do you think that man in the coffee shop was talking about Jake when he said my boyfriend?"

She had no idea why anyone would think Jake had been her boyfriend, but right now that was the only thing that made sense. And that thought chilled her to the bone. Jake worked for a secret agency and now he was gone.

Dead? Of course he was dead. Sam wouldn't say he wasn't coming back if it wasn't true.

And someone had threatened her—worse, they'd actually pushed her last night. The man in the coffee shop had admitted as much. They wanted something from her, but she didn't know what.

Sam looked fierce. "I don't know, but we'll find out."

"I don't see how. Jake's gone, and I don't know who that guy was. Or why he thinks I know anything." She hesitated. "I didn't do anything, Sam. I don't know what's going on and… I'm scared."

He cupped her chin. "I'll keep you safe, Georgie. And I know people who can figure this out."

"I didn't tell you this part, but the man in the coffee shop said that if I didn't want to fall onto the tracks the next time, I'd do what they said. Last night—I thought maybe somebody pushed me. I didn't see who pulled me to safety because people surrounded me then and he was gone so quickly. But I think it was the man from the coffee shop—or somebody associated with him."

Sam's expression darkened. "You didn't tell me you nearly fell on the tracks."

She nodded. "Somebody pulled me away just in time. I was going over the edge and there was nothing to stop me. If they hadn't grabbed me, I'd be dead."

"It's time to get your things, Georgie. And make it quick," he growled.

"Where are you taking me?"

"Somewhere safe."

That wasn't an answer and he knew it. And while she might have no choice in this, there was one place she didn't want to go. "I won't go to Texas, Sam. I can't—"

His fingers caressed her skin again and she found

herself wanting to lean into him, wanting him to keep touching her until the sadness went away. How could her body light up when he touched her even though she was feeling so many other things right now?

"I'm not sending you to Texas. I'm taking you to a friend's house where you'll be safe while I work on this."

A friend's house. She wasn't sure she liked the sound of that. What if he dumped her off and she didn't see him again? "You won't leave me?"

"Only to go to work. I have to show up there. Otherwise I'll be with you."

She looked down at her lap, unable to meet the intensity of his gaze a moment longer. "Okay. I guess I have no choice."

His hand dropped away, and she found herself wanting to cry out, wanting to ask him not to stop.

"No, you really don't. I'm sorry about Sergeant Hamilton, Georgie. But I won't let anything happen to you. You can count on that."

"I know." Impulsively, she reached out and ran her palm along his jaw. She'd been aching to touch him. His eyes darkened, becoming hot pools she wanted to drown in. "I trust you, Sam. Completely. You've always done right by me."

He caught her hand and pulled it away from his face. "You can trust me with your life, Georgie." He kissed her palm and shivers ran down her spine. "But don't make the mistake of thinking you can trust me with anything else. I'm not that good, believe me."

Chapter Six

The trip was silent. Or would have been if not for the incessant meowing of Georgie's cat. Sam was glad Georgie wasn't talking right now. He needed to think. He'd told Big Mac and Kid what was happening earlier.

Big Mac had told him to take Georgie to his place for now and gave Sam a key. They'd figure out what came next once Sam got her settled. He was still processing what Kid had found on Jake Hamilton—and obsessing over the fact that Georgie seemed to be far closer to Hamilton than she was admitting.

Maybe he hadn't been her boyfriend, but that didn't mean something hadn't happened between them.

"You know something, Sam?"

He started at the sound of her voice when the cat had become white noise to him. "What?"

"You said I couldn't trust you with anything else because you weren't that good. But maybe I don't want you to be good. Maybe I want you to be as bad as you can be. Did you ever think of that?"

Sam gripped the wheel and stared straight ahead. *Jesus.* He hadn't fucking expected her to say such a thing. Hell, he didn't know why he'd said those words to her earlier, except that he'd wanted her to know the truth. He wasn't all that good. Not where she was concerned. His control was a finite thing.

And he wasn't about to take advantage of her when she was emotionally compromised by her divorce and the death of Jake Hamilton, whatever that guy might have been to her.

"Don't say shit like that to me, Georgie. You know I'm not going there."

She snorted. "Boy, do I."

"Georgie—"

"No, don't you Georgie me. When you stopped that night..."

He could feel her looking at him, her eyes boring an angry hole into him. His gut twisted. He told himself she was simply reacting to everything that had happened today and taking it out on him. This wasn't really about something that had happened twelve years ago. It was just a convenient target for her chaotic emotions.

The corners of her mouth were white. "When you stopped that night, I thought there was something wrong with me. I thought I wasn't sexy enough or special enough for you. And that hurt."

He blinked. Did she really think...?

"Of course you were," he bit out. "But you're Rick's little sister—and I was the wrong guy for a lot of reasons. I stopped because you *were* special. You *are* special."

She sniffed. "You were the one I wanted."

He swallowed hard. "I couldn't do it, Georgie. I couldn't do it and look Rick in the eye ever again. Or your parents."

She didn't say anything for a long moment. But he could feel the anger rolling off of her. "You know who was my first?"

"Goddamn it, I don't want to know."

His voice snapped in the interior of the car. Even the cat went silent. Sam closed his eyes. He did not lose his temper. Not ever. But she made him forget all the vows he'd ever sworn to himself about controlling his emotions.

Georgie folded her arms over her chest. "Fine. But you know what you need to remember right now? Here it is, so put it front and center in that brain of yours and keep it there. I'm not *your* sister, and I'm not a kid anymore."

Sam sat in stony silence, uncertain what in the hell he could possibly say. No, she wasn't his sister. But it was better if he thought of her that way.

He wanted to keep her in a safe place in his head. But in the space of a conversation she'd gone and thrown her grappling hook over the walls he'd erected and climbed right over them.

She thought he had trouble remembering she wasn't a kid anymore. No, what he had trouble remembering was that he was no good for her. Because damn if he didn't want her. He wanted her every possible way he could have her.

But she wasn't his for the taking. She was too good

for the likes of him. Even if he wanted something more than a few nights of sex with her, he owed the Hayeses too much to drag their daughter into the kind of life he led. Now that he'd joined HOT, his already crazy life had just gotten crazier. His deployments would be more specialized now, more dangerous.

With the Rangers, he'd done plenty of dangerous things—jumping into enemy territory in the middle of the night and engaging in pitched battles with hostile forces while trying to take or defend ground.

But HOT—like Delta Force, the Green Berets, and Navy SEALs—was about a hundred levels up. Their missions were top secret, highly focused, and extremely sensitive. Right now most of their resources were bent toward catching Jassar ibn-Rashad.

The new Freedom Force leader had escaped a mission to capture him just a few months ago. Two men were killed on that mission—Marco San Ramos and Jim Matuzaki. Sam was one of the replacements—Iceman the other—and he felt it keenly.

The other guys didn't talk much about what had happened in the desert, but everyone knew. The entire strike team was captured, and Jim and Marco had been executed when no one would talk.

The rest of them would have been executed too, except that another HOT strike team managed to get them out. Sam hadn't gone on a mission with them yet, but it could happen at any moment.

He hoped it didn't because right now he had Georgie to worry about. When Kid found out that Jake Hamilton had been dragged out of the Potomac only a few days ago, Sam's blood ran cold. Right after that, Georgie called him, terrified, and Sam bolted out of HOT HQ like someone had aimed a flamethrower at his ass.

Thank God he'd been in an unsecure area of the building when she'd called or he wouldn't have had his phone with him. He didn't like to think about what she'd be doing right now if he hadn't been able to take her call for a few hours.

His phone blared to life and he glanced down at it. A HOT code flashed on the screen. He answered with a clipped "McKnight."

"This is Richie. Everything okay?"

Sam's gut hollowed. His new team CO calling him couldn't be a good thing. Matt "Richie Rich" Girard had been nothing other than welcoming, but Sam was still new enough that he didn't quite feel at home yet. He'd get there, though. "Yes, sir. Just have to take care of something personal, sir."

"Leave off the sirs, Knight Rider. We're a team. Big Mac told me about your friend. She okay?"

Sam glanced over at Georgie, who was now staring out the window. Mad at him, no doubt. "I think so, sir— I mean Richie. There was no one in the house, but the back door had been forced and they'd gone through her things. Nothing missing though."

"Glad she's okay. Seems as if circumstances have changed a bit in the last hour," Richie said. "We're officially involved now. You'll need to bring her to HQ, and then we'll make sure she gets to a safe house."

Sam gripped the phone tight. Jesus, if HOT was

involved, there was most certainly a foreign component. The military did not operate inside US borders except under very specific and well-defined circumstances. And that made Sam's blood run just a little colder.

What the hell had Georgie gotten herself into?

"I need to stay with her. I'm responsible for her." Because Rick would kill him if anything happened to Georgie. Hell, Sam would hand him the gun and beg him to pull the trigger.

There was a moment of silence on the other end of the phone. "I think I can arrange it. But get here as fast as you can. Understood?"

"Sir, yes, sir," Sam replied, wincing at how stiff and formal he sounded.

Richie laughed. "You'll get it eventually."

The connection ended and Sam put the phone down again with a sinking feeling in his gut. If HOT was a part of this thing, the level of severity had just taken a quantum leap.

Chapter Seven

GEORGIE STOOD ON THE SCREENED-IN BACK PORCH OF A small cottage on the Eastern Shore of Maryland, arms folded over her chest, staring out at the creek running past the house as a sense of unreality flooded her. It was late afternoon and the sun gleamed golden on the water. A blue heron picked its way along the shore on the opposite side, and marsh grass waved occasionally in the slight breeze called up whenever a bird took flight.

This was not at all what she'd expected to be doing when she woke up this morning. Her head was still reeling from everything that had happened since she'd nearly fallen in front of a train last night—something that had apparently not been an accident.

She heard a sound behind her and turned as Sam strolled outside. He'd changed out of his military uniform and into a pair of faded jeans that sat low on his hips. He wore a navy T-shirt that clung to the broad muscles of his tattooed biceps and chest and made her mouth water.

Tattoos? Sam hadn't had tattoos before. A black tribal design appeared to surround his right bicep. She couldn't tell what was on his left, but she saw a hint of ink when he crossed his arms over his chest.

"You doing okay?"

She shrugged. Belle had calmed down the instant they'd walked inside and she'd been let out to roam the house. Now she was standing on her hind legs, her front paws on the screen, watching the birds in the yard. Her tail swished back and forth happily.

Georgie was anything but happy right now. "I'm a bit out of sorts, actually."

Sam shoved his hands in his pockets and walked over to join her. "Understandable."

After the call in the truck earlier, he'd told her they had to make a stop. She hadn't expected him to drive onto a military facility or up to a compound surrounded by razor wire, but that's exactly what he did. She'd only been allowed inside a big room near the entrance of the compound where they permitted visitors, but it had soon swarmed with large men in uniform who'd gazed down at her with deadly serious expressions. Belle had gone utterly silent in her carrier at that point. Even she'd been intimidated by so much testosterone.

The man with silver birds on his shoulders—thank God for her time with the military so she could at least recognize a colonel now—had held out his hand. "Colonel Mendez, ma'am. You doing okay?"

Everyone wanted to know if she was okay. Hell no, she was *not* okay—but she hadn't told the colonel that. Instead, she'd made some sort of answer, listened while the colonel talked, and then sat down to wait while all the men, including Sam, disappeared into the inner building. A uniformed soldier came back with an offer of coffee, told her she could let Belle out to roam the room if she wanted, and then she was alone again.

Sam didn't return for an hour, but when he did he'd told her they were going to the much quieter Eastern Shore where they would stay for the next few days.

She'd felt so helpless and out of control then.

"I have classes, Sam. I can't just disappear." She winced the moment she said it because it was insensitive after what had happened to Jake.

"The colonel will take care of everything. All you have left is finals, and someone will make sure they're proctored. You'll get the exams to grade. It's non-negotiable, Georgie."

"So it's not just you anymore?" She'd nodded her head toward the giant steel door through which he'd come. "It's all of those guys in there too, right?"

He'd looked somber. "That's right. Jake Hamilton didn't fall into the Potomac by accident."

That was the first she'd heard about how Jake had been found. "So why hasn't it been on the news? A body in the Potomac isn't something you can keep secret for long."

Sam lifted an eyebrow. "Depends on who wants it kept secret."

"I still don't understand why the police aren't involved. Or why the military is."

He'd put his hands on her shoulders. "Because there

are some things the military is better equipped to do. This is one of those things, Georgie."

She'd been thinking about that for hours, and she still had no idea what Jake could have been tangled up in. What was the information those men had wanted from him? And why was she a part of it? What made them think she knew anything at all?

Sam had driven off the base and headed east, eventually rolling over the Chesapeake Bay and onto the Eastern Shore. Another half hour of driving and they'd ended up here, at this small cottage tucked away on a tributary of the bay.

Now Georgie shook her head and voiced what she'd been thinking. "I don't understand why Jake's dead. Or what it has to do with me."

Sam ran a hand through his hair and let out a breath. "Jake was involved in things he shouldn't have been. And it looks like he had a crush on you, G. He had pictures of you in his apartment, poems he'd written. Whoever killed him thinks you know something about what he was doing because they think you were together. Did you go out with him at all?"

"No! And I *don't* know anything. I didn't even know Jake that well. He took three classes from me, that's it. We had coffee a few times, but it was during my office hours. It wasn't a date or anything. I swear."

Jake had been crushing on her? She hadn't known. Then again, he'd come to class early and stayed late a few times. Always talking to her about what they were reading. She'd thought he was just enthusiastic.

"He seemed to think it was a date. He clearly convinced these guys he was seeing you."

She shook her head, wanting to deny everything Sam was saying. "But Jake was a good guy. Harmless. I can't believe he was mixed up in something bad."

"You aren't that naïve, Georgie. Just because someone is nice doesn't mean they haven't done something wrong. I'm sorry when anyone dies so senselessly, but trust me when I tell you he wasn't minding his own business when it happened."

Georgie swallowed the lump in her throat. "So now you get to say when someone deserves the bad things that happen to them? I think that's rather cynical, don't you?"

Sam's expression was stark. "I've seen too much in this life not to be cynical. Jake Hamilton was doing things he shouldn't have been doing. And while I'm sorry you're hurt over this, I'm more pissed that he managed to drag you into it. You're lucky all they wanted to do last night was scare you, otherwise somebody'd be scraping you off the tracks."

She closed her eyes, feeling the ache in her hip anew. Remembering the fear of that moment when she'd been going over the edge. "I know," she whispered. "But I liked Jake. Or at least the Jake I knew. It's not easy to start believing he was a bad person."

"I didn't say he was bad. But he did bad things. Or stupid things, at least. And that cost him his life."

She looked up at him. "And I'm mixed up in it."

Sam nodded. "We don't know exactly how yet. They might think you knew something about what he was doing because he said you were his girlfriend. Or he might have implicated you in some way in order to protect himself. Did he ever give you anything?"

She shook her head. "Tests and papers. Nothing else." She chewed on her bottom lip. "The last time I saw him, he was with a man in the Metro. It was late, and I was waiting for the train home. Jake said he was going to Crystal City with a friend. Then a man showed up and they started talking. I didn't hear what they said."

Sam's gaze sharpened. "And what was unusual in that?"

"I don't know that anything was."

"You mentioned it. I think you wouldn't have done that if it didn't bother you somehow."

Her heart beat a little faster as she thought back to that night. "The man seemed angry. And I didn't like the way he looked at me." She shrugged. "It was nothing else, really. Just a bad feeling he gave me."

"Did you talk to him?"

"No."

"What did he look like?"

"Dark. Middle Eastern maybe, and that pains me to say because it shouldn't mean a damn thing."

"No, it shouldn't. But sometimes it does." He didn't have to remind her that she'd described the man from the coffee shop as vaguely foreign, too.

"He had a goatee, closely cropped. He looked… very manicured. Well-dressed and well-groomed. There was nothing unusual in that, except that he didn't seem to match Jake if you know what I mean. Jake was, I don't know, very casual. Except when in uniform, of course."

"You have something or saw something. Or someone thinks so anyway. And until we figure out what that is, you're staying here."

A little wave of panic rose in her chest. "You aren't leaving me out here alone, are you?" She'd lived alone for the past year, but being left in a remote location in Maryland where she didn't know a soul and couldn't even see the next house? The thought terrified her.

Sam put his hands on her shoulders. "I'm not leaving you. I'm here until this is over. And if I have to leave for some reason, one of the other guys will be with you. We won't leave you unprotected."

Georgie shivered. His hands on her shoulders were warm and strong, and she wanted to feel them everywhere, wanted the heat of him to engulf her. She hated that she did, especially when he seemed so determined to be remote. "Who are those guys?"

"My coworkers," he said, his tone telling her he wouldn't say anything else. "They know what they're doing."

She arched an eyebrow. "Careful, Sam, or I'll start to think you're part of some secret military outfit."

He gazed at her steadily, his expression never changing, and it suddenly hit her that was exactly what was going on. Sam McKnight was a part of something she wasn't supposed to know about.

"Does Rick know?" she asked, and his gaze shuttered.

He turned away from her, his jaw tight. She didn't

know why she felt closer to him in that moment, but she did. He was a part of something big and she was the only one who'd guessed. Even if he wouldn't admit it.

She touched his arm. "I won't say a word. I promise."

"There's nothing to say, Georgie. I'm an Army Ranger. Same as always."

"Of course," she said. But she didn't believe it.

Chapter Eight

SAM WAS RESTLESS AS HELL. EVENING WAS FALLING AND frogs began their nightly chorus against the backdrop of the river and marshes nearby. There was no car noise out here, no planes or motorcycles or people talking. It was peaceful, but he didn't feel at peace.

Georgie sat at the small table on the porch with her laptop. They hadn't spoken much in a couple of hours now. He hadn't known what to say to her, truth be told. Georgie wasn't stupid and of course she would figure there was something going on after he'd taken her to HOT HQ. It wasn't that they didn't bring civilians to HOT—they did, clearly, or there wouldn't be a separate area for visitors—but he hadn't expected to have to take her there.

The cover story was always that they were Rangers when in truth they were so much more. HOT was secret, its members recruited from the Rangers, the Green Berets—and even from Delta Force, which was very similar. The wives of HOT members were briefed, but only with a very minimum of detail.

HOT was, by design, a male-dominated organization. That's just how Special Operations was, though with women being allowed to do combat tours nowadays, he didn't think it would be long before they had female team members too.

Earlier, Sam had gone into the front yard to place a call back to HOT. He'd told them what Georgie had said about the guy with Jake Hamilton. It was probably nothing, but Sam had learned not to discount anything out of hand. Explore every lead, no matter how insignificant.

What he hadn't told Georgie—what he couldn't tell her—was that Jake Hamilton had been attempting to sell information about a DARPA mini-UAV project to a foreign organization. Mini-drones were the size of moths or hummingbirds, and they could do amazing surveillance work. They could also be weaponized, which was a frightening fucking thought.

The problem was powering them for long periods of time. They just didn't have long-range capability. Their juice drained within minutes.

And that's what DARPA was working on. A mini-drone capable of being weaponized and able to fly long distances before recharging. A weapon of that scope in the wrong hands was a nightmare. It could give terrorists a way to attack American troops abroad, and a way to deliver biological agents or dirty bombs to civilian populations.

And if they somehow managed to get the drones into the US? Bad, bad news.

Mendez had said during the briefing that they still didn't know how much information Jake had stolen, but the group he'd been dealing with was apparently a front for the Freedom Force. Mendez didn't think Hamilton had known or cared who he was selling the information to.

He may not have been a particularly stylish dude according to Georgie, but he sure had expensive tastes in things other than clothes. A vintage Corvette, for instance. A rare Colt pistol. Front-row seats to a Gina Domenico concert.

Fucking dumbass. He might have been an admin assistant, but he'd had access to top-secret information because he needed it in order to work for the general. He'd been vetted and cleared—but he'd obviously gotten greedy at some point afterward.

Richie had told Sam to hold tight and they'd get back to him when they had something. Which left Sam with a whole lot of nothing to do except sit around in a remote cottage with the one woman in this world he shouldn't desire.

Georgie looked up from her computer as if she'd known he was thinking about her. Their gazes clashed and held, and his heart ticked up a few beats. He didn't know what to say to her anymore. Hell, he hadn't known what to say to her since the minute she'd walked into that bowling alley in Hopeful and tied his tongue into knots.

He'd been filled with conflicting feelings and he was

still filled with them. She was just about the sexiest woman he'd ever known, and he knew that a lot of that was the lure of the forbidden. He wanted her because he'd decided he couldn't have her.

If she were anyone else, he could fuck her and be done with it. But not Georgie. He wouldn't risk hurting her. If it caused him some discomfort, well, he'd just have to deal with it.

"You hungry?" he asked, getting to his feet and ranging toward the kitchen.

She closed the laptop. "I could use a bite of something."

Sam went over to the fridge and started pulling out vegetables. "Pasta primavera?" he asked when he'd taken inventory of the stocked kitchen. Thank God for HOT's resources. Colonel Mendez had arranged this place at a moment's notice, along with a fully stocked pantry and a generator should they need it.

Georgie came over and leaned against the counter. She was smiling. "Seriously? You can make that?"

He shrugged self-consciously. "I've been on my own for a long time. It was learn to cook or starve."

"Or eat take-out all the time," she added.

"Yeah, that too."

"Can I chop the veggies for you?"

He pushed the pile of vegetables toward her. "Sure."

She began to prepare the veggies while he set up the water to boil and got the butter, cream, and Parmesan from the fridge. The kitchen was small and they had to stand almost elbow-to-elbow. He could feel the heat of her body, smell the perfume of her soap, and his dick started to harden as he imagined her in the shower, water and soap running down her skin.

Why had he let her help him again? Holy Christ, he'd never get through this night with her standing so damn close.

He set the pasta on the counter and walked out of the kitchen.

"Everything okay?" she asked, her voice coming from right behind him.

He sucked in a deep breath and turned around. There she was, looking so vulnerable and tempting as she gazed up at him, her green eyes filled with questions he couldn't begin to answer.

"Yes, fine. I just needed to get something." He didn't have anything in his hands and they both knew it. But she shrugged and went back into the kitchen and he let out a long breath, clenched his fists at his sides, and went to rejoin her.

She finished chopping everything and he put it on to sauté. When he turned around, she'd found a bottle of wine. She held it up. "Want some?"

"I'd better not." He needed to keep his wits sharp and he couldn't do that if he was drinking. Not that he expected anyone to show up here looking for Georgie, but he considered himself on duty. Even if he felt like he wasn't doing a damn thing out here in the boonies.

She removed the cork expertly and poured herself a glass. He watched her take a sip, remembering when she wasn't old enough to drink at all. She used to wrinkle her nose at the beer he and Rick snuck out of her dad's pool-house refrigerator. They hadn't done it often, but when they had, Georgie had never told on them.

She sat on a barstool on the other side of the tiny kitchen counter and smiled at him. His heart hitched in spite of himself.

"So did you think when you came to see me this morning you'd be sharing a house with me tonight?"

"Have to say it was the furthest thought from my mind."

She took another sip of wine. "Yeah, me too. I've pretty much sworn off men altogether, and yet here you are."

He frowned. "I'm sorry Tim hurt you, Georgie."

Her expression tightened. "I think we probably hurt each other. But he's moved on now. Got himself a new fiancée and everything."

He could hear the note of hurt in her voice and it made him want to throttle Tim for her. "Seems kinda quick."

She picked up a sliver of carrot and crunched on it. "You'd think, but it wasn't all that quick after all. Tim and Lindsey have been sharing a bed for a couple of years now."

Sam blinked. "A couple of years? Then that means…" She looked at him expectantly, an eyebrow raised, but he couldn't finish the sentence. Tim Cash had been fucking someone else while still married to Georgie? What an asshole.

"That's right, Tim had a little something on the side." She lifted her glass high. "To Tim and Lindsey, long may they enjoy themselves. God knows they certainly deserve each other."

Sam hated to see her hurting. He especially hated that it was over another man. "I'm really sorry, Georgie. If it helps, and I'm sure it doesn't, Tim's a fucking asshole."

She laughed. "Yeah, he is. But he's not *my* asshole husband anymore, so there's that at least."

"Does your family know?"

She didn't pretend not to understand him. "I've never said as much, but I suspect they have their theories. Besides, I'd rather Rick not charge up here and challenge Tim to pistols at dawn or something."

"I could do it for him. Save him the trip. Plus I'm a better shot."

"Haha, funny man. Forget it. Tim is history." She toyed with the stem of her wine glass. "So why haven't you married yet?"

He ignored the flip of his heart. "Never wanted to."

"You've never been in love?"

He turned away from her and put the pasta in the boiling water, giving it a vicious stir. When he turned back, she was still watching him expectantly. *Fuck*. He didn't quite know what to say. He was thirty-two years old—almost thirty-three—and he'd never been in love. Not only that, but he wasn't sure he believed in love. Or at least not for everyone. His parents damn sure hadn't had it. Neither had Georgie and Tim apparently. Her parents seemed to be in love, but how did anyone really know what went on between two people?

He settled for the truth. "No."

"But you've had girlfriends at least, right?"

"Georgie."

She blinked innocently. "Yes, Sam?"

"Why are you asking me these things?"

"It's called small talk. Remember that?"

Remember? Hell, he wasn't likely to ever forget the last time she'd said that to him. They'd been parked by Hopeful Lake and she'd just told him she wanted him. Not only that, but his cock was beginning to harden at the memory.

He didn't deny himself many things, but when he did he usually accepted it and moved on. Except this time. Perversely, the more he denied himself the right to think about Georgie as anything besides his best friend's little sister, the more he wanted her.

"I remember," he said tightly.

"Sam, I really think you need some wine."

"Why?"

"Because you're too surly, for fuck's sake. And your answers are monosyllabic to say the least. You need to loosen up, relax a bit. We're just old friends catching up again. There's nothing sinister in my questions."

Suddenly, wine didn't seem like such a bad idea. He grabbed a glass from the cabinet. He wouldn't drink much, but a few sips wouldn't hurt him. With his body mass it took a lot to get him drunk. And at least if he appeared to be drinking with her, she might stop asking so many damn questions.

He poured some wine and took a swig. "Happy?"

She smiled. "Getting there."

Chapter Nine

Georgie watched Sam prowl around the kitchen and felt like the annoying kid tagging after the big boys all over again. He clearly didn't want to be cooped up in this house with her, and he damn sure didn't want to talk about anything. What was so damn difficult about saying whether or not he'd ever been in love?

"I'm sorry this is a pain in the ass for you," she finally said when he gave the pasta another sharp twist with the spoon. He glanced at her over his shoulder, then picked up the pot and came over to dump the contents in the strainer. Steam bellowed up from the sink, obscuring his face for a second.

"It's not a pain in the ass. It's just been so damn long since I've seen you that I'm not sure what to say to you anymore."

Georgie could only gape at him. "How can you not know what to say? Aside from today, we haven't seen each other in six years—and that was only while you glared at me and Tim at our reception."

He banged the pan down. "Of course I glared. You were marrying an asshole."

"Well *I* didn't know that," she said primly. "I thought he was wonderful."

Mostly wonderful, she amended in her head. After that aborted night with Sam, she'd gone off to college and had a string of boyfriends she didn't really care about. Then, in her senior year, she'd started going out with Tim, a guy she'd known in high school. He'd been funny and he'd had just enough of that cocky male arrogance to remind her of Sam. Not a good reason to go out with someone, but by the time she'd agreed to marry him, she'd forgotten all about Sam.

Well, mostly forgotten.

"He was always a prick. Too much money, too spoiled, and acted like everyone owed him something."

She nodded. "You won't get an argument out of me these days. Go ahead and trash him all you like. But for a while, I did love him. And I think he loved me."

Sam's gaze snapped to hers, his dark eyes glittering hot. "Of course he did. He'd have been a fool not to."

Astonishment ricocheted through her. "Why, Sam, are you complimenting me?"

"Is that so hard to believe?"

She took another drink of her wine. "Well, I don't know. You've pretty much frowned and growled at me since I turned fifteen."

He looked thoughtful. "Have I?"

"Hell, you even frowned that night out at Hopeful Lake. If there was ever a moment *not* to frown, that would have been it. Or do you always look like that when you're about to have sex with a woman you've taken home for the night?"

"Jesus, Georgie. Why do you keep reminding me about that night?"

She shrugged. "It's pretty much the last time I had any interaction with you. And it was memorable, you have to admit. Though it could have been more so."

He turned back to the stove with a growl and she shook her head. "I'm beginning to think you're a prude, Sam. Every time I mention anything to do with sex, you can't shut me down fast enough."

He brought the vegetables and sauce over to the counter and tossed the pasta into the pan, mixing it with short jerking motions of the skillet. "I don't want to talk about this kind of stuff with you, that's why. I'm not a prude, but it's none of your business."

She was getting mad now and she didn't quite know why. "It *was* my business when you had your hand between my legs and your tongue down my throat."

He dished some pasta onto a plate and set it in front of her. "That was twelve years ago, and I'm not discussing it with you."

Fury and hurt warred for space inside her. "I'm sick of you treating me like I can't make any decisions for myself. It was *my* choice to give you my virginity, and though it was your choice not to take it, you can't pretend it never happened. It *would* have happened if you weren't such a damned uptight son of a bitch—"

His head snapped up. The look he gave her was so full of menace that the words died in her throat. "Is that what you think? Is that what you honestly fucking think?

That I pushed you away because I was being a son of a bitch? Because I didn't respect your *choice?*"

He leaned toward her then, until he was nearly in her face. "I respected you and your family too much to do that to you, Georgie. To screw you in the front seat of a beat-up truck out by the lake when you deserved diamonds and silk and champagne?" He shook his head, hard. "No fucking way. You were trying to be a rebel and trying to use me to do it. And that's not a good enough reason."

She sat back in her chair, stunned. His words rang in her ears. *Diamonds and silk and champagne.* "You thought I was using you to rebel?"

He dumped pasta on a plate for himself. "Why else? You could have had anyone, but you chose me. Your parents were good to me, but do you think they'd have been thrilled to know their little princess was out fucking the boy who, only by the grace of God and their good influence, wasn't as much of a loser as he was destined to be?"

"You've got it all wrong, Sam. Every bit of it." She could barely push the words past the tightness in her throat.

He glared at her. "Have I? You wanted me because I was wrong for you, because I was the bad boy. You spent years building up that fantasy in your head. I saw it every time you looked at me."

She'd known when they'd been kids that he'd been lonely and sad, but she hadn't known he'd felt like he was bad. How could he be bad? He'd been a part of their family, and her parents weren't poor judges of character. Oh, he'd gotten into trouble here and there—but never anything serious, and never anything that lasted for long.

He *had* been expelled once, but her dad had gone and had a long talk with the principal—and Sam was back in school again. She'd never doubted his character for one minute.

"I wanted you because you made my heart sing. Yes, I was infatuated with you. I spent years being infatuated with you. None of it had anything to do with you being a bad boy. Were you a bad boy? I didn't know it. All I knew was you were there, in my house, looking handsome and broody and sexy. You played guitar and sang, and you were nice to me—when you weren't telling me what to do. I adored you for those reasons, no other. When you came home again, I was so certain you'd finally see me as a woman, not Rick's annoying little sister. Yes, I came after you and I wanted you to be my first—hell, I probably wanted you to be my only, but I did have a healthy fantasy life back then and the idea of marrying you and moving from Army base to Army base seemed like an adventure." She shrugged to cover her discomfort. "I'm sorry if you felt like I was using you. It was the furthest thing from my mind, believe me."

He was staring at her. "It's post."

"I'm sorry?" She'd said all that, and all he could say was something nonsensical?

"Army post. It's an Air Force base. An Army post."

She picked up her fork and twisted it into the pasta as if she had no cares in the world. Inside, she was trembling. She'd just bared some of her most private feelings to him and he was treating it like it was nothing.

"Well, I'll have to remember that. Thanks for the lesson."

"Georgie."

She looked up. He reached over and took her free hand in his. Squeezed. "I'm sorry I disappointed you. I was trying to protect you."

"It's not your job to protect me, Sam."

He gave her a lopsided grin that made her heart stutter. "Actually, it is. Right now anyway."

"I appreciate that, really. But it only applies to this situation with Jake and those men, not to anything else. Please remember that."

"I'll try."

"Good."

He blew out a breath. "I wasn't right for you then. I hope you realize that. I wasn't in a good place, and I didn't want to hurt you."

"You might not have wanted to, but you did anyway. Self-esteem can be a fragile thing at that age and you shattered mine pretty badly when you pushed me away."

"I was trying to do the right thing."

"I know that now." She took a bite of pasta to cover her raw nerves. "Oh my God, this is good. So much better than sex."

It wasn't a good segue, but it would have to do. Because it didn't do any good to talk about the past with Sam. She still felt like the annoying little kid.

And the fact that he'd been trying to protect her

when he'd turned her away twelve years ago? It only made her heart squeeze a little tighter and her emotions twist into knots.

Sam shook his head and laughed. "Now you're just trying to bait me into saying something contradictory."

"Maybe." She took another bite and closed her eyes. "Or maybe not. Seriously, who needs a man when you have this? It's an orgasm on a plate."

"You're laying it on a little thick, G."

She grinned at him. "So you think. But really, sex is a bit overrated. Even you have to admit that. We get all worked up based on our hormones—and then what? It feels nice for a while and then it's over." She shrugged. "I've been living without it for over a year now and I'm no worse off."

Intense dark eyes raked over her face and something throbbed deep inside her. Suddenly, sex seemed a whole lot more important than she wanted it to be.

"Eat the pasta, G, and shut the hell up."

"You're growling again," she said.

He only glared at her.

Chapter Ten

THERE WAS A THUNDERSTORM LATER THAT NIGHT. The crack of thunder and sizzle of ozone woke Georgie up. She bolted up in bed, feeling disoriented until she remembered where she was. Sam was on a fold-up Army cot in the living room. He'd given her the bed and stationed himself in the small room right off the front door. She didn't ask if he was armed. She didn't have to.

He must have seen the concern on her face because he'd told her it was simply SOP—standard operating procedure. He didn't expect a threat, but he prepared for one because that's what he did.

She'd gone to bed feeling only marginally better since she suspected he wouldn't tell her the truth anyway. There could be a whole boatload of bad guys out there and he wouldn't let her know it. Except she had to admit that she was pretty confident in the men she'd met earlier today. They were on top of this, whatever this was, and they'd find the person—or people—who'd killed Jake.

Thunder cracked again, and Belle scrambled under the bed. Georgie threw the covers back and went into the bathroom. When she came out, she realized she'd finished the bottle of water she'd set on her bedside table so she went into the kitchen to get another one.

She could see Sam lying on the cot, one arm thrown over his face, the other beside him. Lightning flashed and illuminated the room for a split second, and Georgie had to stifle the groan on her lips.

God, he was beautiful. He lay on top of the covers, clad in a pair of shorts, and his bare chest was a sight to behold. Far more muscular than when he'd been seventeen—or even twenty-one. And he was inked. She couldn't tell what the designs were in that brief flash of light, but she'd seen them there and they made her mouth go dry.

What would it be like to trace them with her tongue? Wetness flooded her at the thought, and her temperature kicked up a degree. She'd told him sex was overrated—and she hadn't been kidding—but what if it wasn't overrated with him? What if he possessed the ability to make her feel something more than just the sweetness of a release?

Georgie shivered with awareness. It had been so long since a man had touched her. So long since she'd cared. And now here she was, panting over the one man who had always seemed determined not to have anything to do with her.

She crept toward the cot. She just wanted to see him up close, wanted to know if the ripple of muscle was as impressive as it had seemed in that flash of light.

Wanted to see him breathing and know he was really here and that she wasn't somehow imagining the whole thing in a fevered dream.

"What are you doing?"

His voice startled her. She stopped, clutching her water bottle, and swallowed. "Just making sure you're okay."

He removed his arm from over his face. She could see the glitter of his eyes in the darkness. "I'm fine."

He sounded prickly as usual, and it got to her. "Your virtue is safe with me, Sam. You don't have to get all edgy about it. I wasn't coming over to take advantage of you or anything."

He swung his legs to the floor and sat up. "I'm not worried about my virtue."

"No, you're worried about mine. Or about what Rick or my parents would think if you did what you really want to do."

He tilted his head to the side. "How do you know what I really want to do? Maybe I'm not attracted to you. Did you ever consider that?"

She felt those words like a blow. After everything with Tim, after the heartbreak and betrayal, the idea that yet another man found her less than appealing hurt more than she could say.

Yes, she'd done it to herself. She'd poked and prodded and pushed—and for what? So he could tell her he didn't want her? So she could suffer the sting of humiliation yet one more time?

Georgie couldn't think of one damn thing to say. Instead, she turned on her heel and fled toward the bedroom. She was inside, throwing the door closed, when a big shape wedged itself between the door and the jamb. She didn't fight. She just let go and stepped back, arms around herself as he loomed big in the room.

Thunder crashed harder than before, but she didn't take her attention from Sam.

"Goddamn you, Georgie," he said softly. "You push and push and push, and then when I push back, when I try like hell to keep you from making a mistake, I say something so fucking rotten even I can't believe I said it." He shook his head. "I'm sorry, I didn't mean it. You're beautiful and hot, and any man would be crazy not to want you."

She held up a hand. "Stop. I don't want to hear another word. You don't mean it. I know you're just trying to make me feel better. And it's my fault for putting you in that position. I do keep pushing, and I don't know why. Maybe it's Tim and the marriage…" Here she actually had to swallow down a load of tears. "…And the humiliation of being left for someone else. I don't know, but you have my word I won't do it again."

His voice, when he spoke, was low and hoarse, as if it were being dragged from him. "I do want you, Georgie. I've wanted you since that night twelve years ago. I want to spread you out beneath me and make you come so many times you can't do it anymore. I want to taste your pussy and feel your legs wrapped around me as I pound into you. I want to see you swallow my cock and hear you cry out in ecstasy. I want all those things, and the only reason I don't take them is because you deserve better. I can't give you anything, Georgie. I'm nothing, nobody—"

She closed the distance between them and put her hand over his mouth, trembling with anger and something more.

Desire. Want. Need.

"Shut up, Sam. Shut the fuck up right now. You *are* somebody. To *me*. You always have been. I've loved you since I was thirteen, and I'm not an idiot. Rick loves you. My parents love you. None of us are stupid."

She was crying now, the tears flowing freely down her cheeks. She put her hands on either side of his face, cupped his hard jaw with shaking fingers. "You aren't a nobody. You're amazing and wonderful and perfect just the way you are. And if your parents couldn't see that, if they made you think differently, then you need to believe me and not them. Because I'm right, dammit, and they're the ones who're stupid."

He spanned the back of her head with one broad hand. She could feel the tremors running through his body as he held her there. "You're so fucking sweet, Georgeanne. I've always wanted you, since I first noticed you grew breasts. I've had a helluva time keeping my hands off you all these years. But I had to do it. You were meant for more than I could give you, and I couldn't disrespect your parents that way. They trusted me. I couldn't break that trust."

Her breasts were tingling, her nipples tightening, and her core had grown impossibly wet. "They aren't here now," she said, stepping into his big body, bringing her aching breasts in contact with his naked chest. The thin cotton of her pajama top wasn't much of a barrier, but it felt like the most torturous wall between them at the moment. "And even if they were in the next room, they have no say in my life. Nor should they have a say in yours. We're adults, Sam. We do what we want. With whom we want."

"I know that, but—"

She put her hand over his mouth to stop him from talking, from ruining this moment. She needed this. Needed him. So damn much. She'd felt empty for so long, and here was this man who made her feel like a sexual being again. Like she was made of lightning and flame.

"No one is here but you and me, and no one ever has to know if that's what you really want. What I want is you—inside me, making me come. Making me feel like I'm beautiful again. Like I'm worth wanting."

She didn't think he would do anything, but then he lowered his head slowly, almost as if he were fighting himself. Right before he kissed her, he muttered against her mouth, "Tim was a fucking idiot, do you hear me? *No* woman is more beautiful than you."

Chapter Eleven

HE WAS DAMNED. HE KNEW IT, AND HE DIDN'T REALLY care right this moment. Georgeanne Hayes was in his arms, her pretty body pressed tight against his, and he didn't fucking care about anything else.

Her mouth parted beneath his and his tongue slipped inside, drawing her into a delicious stroking that made his body harder than it already was. She said he was worthwhile, important, and he believed her.

For right now anyway, he believed her.

He'd fought himself twelve years ago, and he'd fought himself today—Jesus, was it just today?—and he wasn't fighting anymore. Georgie knew what she wanted and he was going to give it to her at least once before he died. He couldn't have her permanently because his life was too unpredictable, but he could have this.

He'd spent the day worrying over her safety, wondering what her relationship with Jake Hamilton had been before she'd insisted there'd been nothing between them, and imagining what would have happened if those assholes had really meant for her to die last night.

She wouldn't be here in his arms, so vibrant and alive and willing.

Georgie's hands roamed over his hot flesh and then slid beneath his shorts until she grasped him. He groaned softly, his body so hard it hurt. Her hand was small and soft as she stroked him and pleasure began to sing inside his brain. He felt the familiar tightening at the base of his spine and knew he had to stop her before he embarrassed himself and spilled in her hand.

He broke the kiss and pushed her back until he could pull off her little pajama top and matching shorts. Her curves beckoned, a banquet for his hands and eyes and mouth.

"Oh, Georgeanne, the things I want to do to you," he said, his voice a soft sizzle in the night.

"Don't talk about it, Sam. Just do it."

"Remember you asked for it," he said, pushing her back onto the bed and coming down on top of her. He nipped her earlobe, slid his tongue along the column of her throat, and then fastened his mouth around one tight nipple while she gasped and arched herself into him.

Her fingers clutched his shoulders, dug into his muscles, and he loved the feel of it. Loved that she clung to him, making little noises while he sucked her nipple. He alternated the pressure, a little soft, a little hard, finding just the right amount she liked. Then he moved to her other nipple and repeated the performance.

He slid a hand down her smooth skin, came to the

mound of her sex—and found it clean-shaven. He nearly choked on his own tongue at that little discovery. He could feel her panting and, yes, even laughing a little.

"Not what you expected?"

He left her breasts and trailed his mouth down her abdomen. "No. It's very naughty of you, G. Very sexy."

"I'd tell you I did it for you, but that would be a lie. I did it for me. Because I wanted to, because I like the way it looks and feels. It's the only thing that's made me feel sexy these past few months."

He reached her mound and placed a kiss there. "You are sexy. Incredibly sexy." He ran a finger down the seam of her pussy. "So hot and wet, Georgie. What do you want me to do about it?"

"I want you inside me."

"All in good time."

Because he wasn't stopping now. Once before, he'd managed to step back from the brink. Not this time. This time he was doing it all. Every little thing he'd been dreaming about.

He pushed her legs open and settled between them. And then he ran his tongue the length of her pussy while she cried out.

She tasted like honey to him—sweet, sweet honey. He spread her open with his fingers and licked his way around her slick folds. And then he touched the point of his tongue to her clit and she arched up off the bed with a sharp cry. He held his tongue against her while she writhed, stunned that she'd come so quickly.

When her tremors subsided, he built the tension

again, this time adding his fingers to the mix, sliding in and out of her with short, hard strokes. She shattered again, his name a broken sound on her lips.

It was the most beautiful sound he'd ever heard, and he'd heard a lot of women say his name in bed. But none of them were Georgie.

He kissed his way up her body, his hands gliding over her sweet soft skin, learning her by touch, mapping her for his memory so that he could call up these moments when she was out of his life again. So he could remember how it felt to make love to Georgeanne Hayes.

"You'd better not be planning to leave now that you've made me come," she gasped.

Her skin was slick with perspiration, and he laughed low in his throat. "Oh no, not this time. I'm too hungry for you."

Too far gone.

"Thank God for small favors."

He levered up and yanked off his shorts and underwear. He reached into the bedside table and knew he'd find condoms. Leave it to HOT to think of everything. He tore one open and rolled it on. He could hear Georgie breathing rapidly, and he leaned down to kiss her.

"I don't want to hurt you," he said.

"I doubt you're *that* big."

He couldn't believe that she could make him laugh at a time like this. "I'm thinking of your hip, smartass."

"I'll let you know, but right now I think it hurts worse not to have you where I want you."

He sucked a nipple into his mouth again, held himself over her, his cock just nudging her slick folds. He wanted to plunge home and keep plunging until he was nothing but a mass of raw nerve endings. But more than that, he didn't want to hurt her already-bruised body.

"Sam, please. I've been waiting twelve years. Longer if you consider when I first knew what sex was about."

"All the more reason to take our time." He slid just inside her, held steady while she writhed beneath him. "You're hot, Georgie. So fucking hot. It's everything I can do to do this right."

"There is no right way or wrong way. There's only you and me and this amazing feeling that I'll die if you don't make me come again."

He slid just a little deeper. "I thought you said sex was overrated."

"It still might be. But I won't know until you actually do something."

Sam shook his head even as his balls began to ache with the need to plunge into her. "I thought I did do something. Didn't you just come?"

"Yeah, and I'm greedy for more." She sucked in a breath and he could hear the tears in her voice. "I've felt undesirable to anyone for so long I almost forgot how good it could feel to have a man in my bed."

He kissed her. "Shh, Georgie, it's all right. I'm not leaving until you're completely satisfied."

She lifted her hips and tried to get him to go deeper. He gave her a little more length. She curled a leg around his hip.

"Is this the injured one?" he asked, hooking his arm behind her knee.

"No."

"Good." He pushed her leg up until it was brushing his shoulder, opening her wide. And then he sank the rest of the way inside her.

"Oh my God, that's good," she gasped.

He held himself still, afraid he'd lose it if he didn't. "Yeah."

He couldn't manage another word. He was deep inside Georgeanne Hayes, the perfect little princess of his teenage years—and he wanted to corrupt her utterly. He wanted to possess her and make her scream his name. He wanted to imprint himself on her so thoroughly she'd never forget this night with him.

He turned his head and pressed a kiss to her calf. He could feel her inner muscles gripping him, urging him forward, but he held still and just enjoyed the feeling of being inside her at long last.

Lightning flashed outside the window, and her face was illuminated for a second. Her head was thrown back, her eyes closed, her lower lip between her teeth. She looked utterly beautiful and completely lost in the moment.

"Look at me," he commanded, because he couldn't stand for her to be lost in her own world without him. He needed that touchstone, needed to see her eyes and know she was with *him*, with Sam McKnight, and not just the first man to touch her since Tim Cash had broken her heart.

Her eyes snapped open and the lightning flashed

again. He saw exactly what he was looking for—raw need, all for him. He began to move, pulling out of her slowly, slamming back in just a little harder each time.

"Oh," she said, again and again. "Oh *yessss*."

Sam rocked into her faster, harder, deeper. Intensely. He let go of her leg, changed the angle at which he entered her, and listened to her beg him for yet more. He was mindless, a machine, a creature who existed solely to pleasure this one woman. He wanted her sighs and moans, her breathy gasps, her screams. He wanted everything she had to give, and he would do anything to get it.

His body was on fire with sensation. All his pleasure centered on his balls, his cock, on the slick pressure of Georgie's body surrounding him. He couldn't remember the last time it had been this good, though it must have been. He loved sex, loved pleasuring a woman, and loved the ultimate payoff when he finally let himself go.

But he couldn't for the life of him recall it feeling quite this good before.

Georgie arched up off the bed and tugged his head down for a kiss, a hot, wet melding of tongues that was not unlike the melding of their bodies. He sucked her tongue into his mouth, nipping her lower lip.

"Sam—oh God, Sam. Please, please… I need…"

He knew what she needed. What he needed.

He withdrew from her body, urged her up and onto her knees. She bent over and gripped her pillow, her ass in the air, and Sam couldn't help but take a moment to run his fingers over her naked folds. So pretty, so hot. Georgie whimpered then and he positioned himself, plunging deep inside her. The angle was different here, but still so good. He loved the sight of his body disappearing into hers, the sounds their bodies made as he rocked into her.

He ran a finger over her clit and felt her shiver. He skimmed it again and again, enjoyed the way she worked her body against his fingers, seeking more pleasure. Her inner muscles tightened, clamping him almost painfully as the pressure built inside her. He could feel her release beginning and he pumped into her harder. At the last second, his thumb skimmed the tight bud of her anus, pressing ever so lightly on that most sensitive of spots.

She flew apart with a long cry, his name a sob as her body shuddered and bucked against him. He pushed her forward against the mattress even more, pushing her thighs together until his were on the outside of hers. She gripped him so tightly it was almost painful as he drove into her again and again, until the pressure in his balls just frigging exploded. He came hard, his body flying apart, dissolving.

When he came back to himself, he was on top of Georgie, who was sprawled against the mattress now, his cock still deep inside her, still twitching as her inner walls spasmed against him from time to time. They were both panting and sweating and the storm was still raging outside, though farther away now.

He pushed himself up and off her. He wanted nothing more than to collapse and sleep for the next fourteen hours or so, but he had to remove the condom. He got up and went into the bathroom and when he came back, he hesitated. She was still on her belly, still sprawled across the mattress, and he suddenly felt like an asshole for using her so roughly.

He'd fucked her dirty, as if she'd wanted it that way when he knew nothing of the sort, and he wished he could start over, do it right this time. She was too precious, too special to treat so casually.

She turned her head, saw him standing there, and rolled onto her side. Her body glistened in the moonlight that streamed into the room now that the storm had moved on. She was curvy, perfectly made, and he wanted to fall to his knees and worship her, beg her forgiveness for daring to use her for his pleasure.

"That," she said softly, "was fucking *amazing*."

Chapter Twelve

Georgie's body ached, but in a good way. Oh, her hip was pretty sore, but she wouldn't trade a moment of what had just happened for less pain. She frowned as she realized Sam was staring at her in that way of his that never meant well for her in the end. He was brooding about something when all she wanted was to wrap herself around him and go to sleep for a few hours so she could wake up and do it all over again.

"I was too rough," he said brusquely. "I should have taken better care of you."

Georgie pushed herself to a sitting position. "What, are you kidding me? Did you just hear a word I said?"

He was standing there, not moving, and she took the opportunity to let her gaze slide over his naked body.

Oh. My. God.

He was beautiful, big and muscled, with tattoos on his chest and biceps. His abs were tight and defined, his hipbones made her want to bite them, and his cock was still half-hard.

And completely beautiful. She didn't have tons of experience with men—oh, she'd been to college and she'd been married to Tim, but no lover she could remember had been quite as satisfying. Sam knew how to use his body to get the most out of hers, that was for sure.

"You don't have to pretend, Georgie. I was rough with you."

"If that was rough, I want it again just as soon as possible."

He came over and stood beside the bed, his eyes on hers. "You aren't just saying that?"

She got up on her knees and put her palms against his chest. "Sam, my God, no."

She slid her hands over him, felt the smooth ridges of muscle, the nicks and dings of scar tissue where he'd been injured. She was so damned emotional right now and it was all because of him. Because she'd felt like there was something wrong with her, like she wasn't all that desirable. Tim had left her for another woman. How could she not take that personally? How could she not think there was something wrong with *her* response in bed? If she couldn't satisfy Tim, who had fairly vanilla tastes, what did that say about her?

But then Sam had just made love to her in ways that were a revelation. He hadn't treated her like a princess on a pedestal. He'd treated her like a woman with earthy tastes and needs, and she'd loved every moment of it. He hadn't been rough, or even particularly kinky—he'd just been wrapped up in the moment, and so had she.

And she damn well wanted more of the same.

"Don't lie, Georgie. Because if you don't tell me the truth, I'll do it again. I'll start out wanting to be gentle, wanting to take you carefully, and I'll end up forgetting and just taking you however I feel like."

She shivered. "Oh wow, I sure hope so."

He closed his eyes and tilted his head back and she pressed her mouth to his pec. She hadn't gotten to taste him earlier, and she'd desperately wanted to. His skin was hot, salty, and she ran her tongue down to his nipple, swirling around it.

His breath hissed in. "You're making me hard."

Her stomach hollowed with need. "Oh goodie. Because I want you again, Sam. I need you to make me come as many times as possible in one night."

WHEN GEORGIE WOKE AGAIN, the sun was up and Sam was gone. She could hear him banging around in the kitchen so she wasn't worried. She stretched, her body rippling with satisfaction.

Sam was a force to be reckoned with in bed. And she was surprised to learn that she wasn't far behind. She wanted to experience everything with him. She wanted his passion, his incredible body, his intense focus. When Sam made love to her, he committed himself fully to the act.

His tongue and teeth were magic—as were his fingers, his cock, and the way he just knew how to touch her or move inside her at precisely the right moment. He'd made her scream his name too many times to count. He'd talked dirty to her when she'd tentatively asked him to.

She hadn't been sure if he would—or even if she would like it—but my God, the way her body clenched when he whispered that he was going to fuck her hard and fast. She'd shattered with little more incentive than those words and his body deep inside hers.

She was, she was discovering, adventurous and enthusiastic. It was such a revelation after the last several years that she wanted to call Tim and Lindsey and tell them to kiss her ass.

She wouldn't, of course, because ladies did not act that way. She stifled a giggle when she thought of her beauty-queen mother instructing her on proper etiquette and the ways in which a true lady behaved.

A true lady probably didn't ride her lover's cock with abandon or beg him to suck her nipples harder while she came either. Both of those were things that Georgie had done last night.

And she wasn't sorry for it, either.

She got up and went into the bathroom, brushed her teeth, and took a very quick shower before slipping into a maxi dress and piling her hair on top of her head. When she went into the kitchen in search of coffee, Sam was there, his back to her, scrambling eggs and fixing toast, and her heart just sort of melted.

He was shirtless and he had a tribal tattoo that spread from his shoulder to the small of his back. She hadn't noticed last night because she hadn't exactly been looking there.

"Wow, that must have hurt," she said.

He glanced at her, and her heart sort of skipped a little bit. He didn't look like he was cutting himself away from her, but he didn't look as open as he had in bed either. She knew what he was thinking about. Or she thought she knew.

In the broad light of day, he'd be thinking pretty hard about her family and how it was some kind of a betrayal to sleep with her. Which was ridiculous considering they were adults and this wasn't the Middle Ages, but it was still so much like Sam to be concerned about her family. She wanted to kiss him senseless and smack him silly at the same time.

And then she wanted to wrap herself around him and never let go.

That thought gave her pause because it was pretty intense. Yeah, she'd been in love with him once but she'd done a whole lot of living since then. She wasn't the same naïve girl she used to be, and love wasn't something she could ever approach with the same innocence she once had. She'd been burned by it too badly.

Besides, you couldn't be in love with a man you'd barely spoken to in twelve years, even if he had given you pretty much the best sex of your life. She loved him as a friend. Always had, always would.

"Things worth having often hurt. And yeah, tattoos fucking hurt."

"So why do it?"

He shrugged. "Because I wanted to."

"Sounds like a good enough reason to me."

He turned around and set a plate with eggs and

toast on the counter in front of her. "You all about doing things because you want to do them now?"

He was mocking her, so she stuck her tongue out at him. She didn't miss the way his eyes darkened or the way her pulse kicked up in response. "I'm a free spirit, Sam. I go where the wind blows me."

"Where's it blowing you today?"

She arched an eyebrow. "I think it'll blow me to my laptop to grade papers. Then it'll blow me outside for a look at the water, maybe a short walk. Then it'll probably blow my clothes right off."

"You planning to be inside or outside when that happens?"

She shrugged. "Depends, I guess."

"On what?"

"On where you are in relation to me and how badly I need your cock inside me."

He closed his eyes and swallowed. "Georgie, when you say things like that…"

"Makes you hard, right?"

"Makes me fucking crazy. Makes me want things…"

"What kind of things?"

He poured some coffee and set it near her plate. "Eat your eggs, Georgie."

She forked some into her mouth and swallowed. "You're a mess, Sam McKnight. But you sure are a hot mess."

He grinned at her and her heart kicked. "Takes one to know one."

Chapter Thirteen

SHE WAS DRIVING HIM CRAZY. SAM DIDN'T REMEMBER ever being so wound up over a woman in his life, though he knew that a large part of it was the fact she was Georgeanne Hayes and he'd decided a long time ago she was off-limits to him.

He was having a hard time remembering why he'd decided such a thing when he replayed the two of them in bed together last night, but then he remembered why they were here in this cottage. She was in trouble and he was supposed to be protecting her—and that made him remember why his kind of life wasn't right for a woman like her.

He didn't want Georgie in danger. Not ever. Not that she would be with him, but it was such a part of his life that it would touch her in ways he didn't want to contemplate. What if they were together and something happened to him? What then?

Hell, he didn't need to be thinking about this. It was

just sex and it was going nowhere. Last night happened because she was his friend and she was still hurting from her divorce. He shouldn't have touched her—but when he'd realized how upset she was at what he'd said, he'd been unable to stop himself. She'd been so wounded and vulnerable, and he'd just wanted her to know that she was perfect in his eyes.

Tim Cash was a douche bag. How could he screw around on a woman like Georgie? He'd had everything and he'd fucked it up. Sam couldn't imagine how Tim could have wanted another woman when he'd had Georgie in his bed.

Jesus. A part of Sam wanted to rewind the clock and take back everything that had happened last night so he wouldn't feel this damn guilt wrapping around him when he thought of explaining what he'd done to Rick.

"I'm worried about her, Sam. Can you check on her?"

"Sure thing, bro. While I'm at it, I'll fuck her for good measure."

Sam gritted his teeth. Yeah, like that's what he'd say to her brother.

But it's how he felt. Like he'd betrayed their friendship in some way when he'd used Georgie for his own gratification.

Yet he still wanted to strip her down to her bare skin and lay her out on the nearest flat surface so he could touch and taste and feel his way to bliss one more time. She'd rocked his world last night, and not just because she said things that shocked him—because she was Georgie and she was supposed to be prim and proper—

but also because she was so honest and real with her feelings. She believed in him, and that both terrified him and buoyed him at the same time.

Not many people in his life had ever believed in him. The Hayeses had, but he had to imagine they wouldn't be pleased about him and Georgie. Not that there was a him and Georgie. Still, he knew what kind of life she was supposed to have, what kind of life they wanted her to come back to Texas for.

Georgie was meant to be lording it over the Junior League while tending her three perfect children, maintaining her McMansion in the right part of town, and making love to her happy husband every night.

Jesus, and wasn't that just a perfectly sexist thought?

He tossed in an image of Georgie as a CEO, put the handsome and happy husband at home in an apron, and felt much better about the whole thing. Well, not better, but more politically correct anyway. So long as it ended with Georgie in Hopeful—or Dallas or Austin, maybe—everything would come out right.

"I expect you're thinking about my family again," she said from behind him.

He turned and leaned back against the counter, watching her eat. Her hair was piled on her head, exposing the slender column of her neck. Her creamy skin had marks that he'd put there, and it filled him with a male satisfaction that was hard to deny. They weren't dark marks, or even very noticeable. But he knew.

"Hard not to. Rick asked me to check on you, not take you to bed and do dirty things to you."

She grinned. "And how I loved those dirty things. You can be dirty with me anytime, handsome."

Sam shook his head. "What would your mother say if she heard you talk like that?"

"Mother believes that a woman should know her mind—and demand what she wants out of life."

"Somehow I doubt that extends to hot sweaty sex with tattooed soldiers."

She lifted an eyebrow. "And how would you know? For all we are aware, she loves hot sweaty sex. And tattooed soldiers."

Sam shook his head. "Do not put that image in my mind. Your mother is a goddess who wears pearls to breakfast and gloves to garden parties."

Georgie was laughing. "Trust me, I could barely say it. But it *was* funny. You have to admit it."

He couldn't help but grin. "Yeah, fine. But we'll leave it at that. No more mom jokes."

She sipped her coffee. "I doubt I have another one in me anyway. Mother is a paragon of propriety."

He nodded. "Yep, she sure is…" He thought of Mrs. Hayes with her delicate features, her perfect hair and perfect smile, her warm hugs, and the way she'd patiently taught him to be a gentleman without once making him feel inadequate about the things he hadn't known.

Georgie wasn't her mother—but she still had her mother's grace. "So what is it you want out of life, Georgie? Because your family seems to think you're up here brooding about your divorce."

"I am not brooding." She put her fork down on the edge of the plate. "I like it here. Or I did until yesterday when things went to shit in my life through no fault of my own."

"I'm sorry, G. I hated having to tell you that Jake Hamilton was dead."

"I know." She smiled sadly. "The truth is I like what I do in my job, and I really like what you and I did last night. I'd like more of that. For right now, that's what I want."

He was all about more of last night. He shouldn't be, but he was. And he was damned glad to hear she wanted it too.

"What we did last night was pretty spectacular to me too. It felt great, and I'd be lying if I said I didn't want more of the same."

"So don't say anything to ruin it."

He frowned. "I wasn't going to. But, Georgie, if you're thinking there's more to this than sex—there's not."

Because he had to be truthful even if it cost him another night with her naked body wrapped around his.

She rolled her eyes. Not quite the reaction he'd been expecting. "Oh for God's sake. I should have never told you I'd imagined marrying you twelve years ago. That was a fantasy born of my youthful naïveté. I'm not that young or idealistic anymore. I'm capable of meaningless sex, Sam."

Meaningless? Why didn't he like that word?

"That's good to know. Because I have a crazy job, G.

I can be here one minute and gone the next, and no idea when I'll be back again. You don't want to be a part of that."

"I'll decide what I want to be a part of, thanks." She picked up the fork again and finished the last bite of eggs. "But don't worry that I'm trying to turn last night into happily ever after. I had my taste of that fantasy, with the big wedding and the till-death-do-us-part bit, and I know it doesn't work out."

For some reason, it saddened him to hear her say that. Georgie was supposed to be the optimistic one. But she'd been burned, and it couldn't help but affect her.

Her phone rang. They'd had a debate at HOT HQ about her keeping it, but they'd decided it might be a good idea in case Jake's contact called and told her what they wanted from her. Since the terror cell was currently under surveillance, they wouldn't be able to move undetected—which meant they weren't tracking her to this location without a lot of warning.

Small comfort to Sam, but at least it was something.

Georgie glanced at the screen. Then she groaned. "It's Rick," she said.

Sam felt a pinch in his chest. Maybe he shouldn't, but he did.

"Hey, big bro," she said, answering the phone brightly. Sam couldn't stay and listen to her talk to her brother so he grabbed his own phone and went outside on the back deck. The day was still early and the sun sparkled on the water. A blue heron stood in the shallows, one foot raised, so still it looked like a statue.

Sam dialed HOT. Big Mac answered. "Hey, Knight Rider. Just planning to call you."

His heart thumped. "Yeah? Got anything?"

"Kid's pulled up some video surveillance from the Metro for the last night she saw Jake Hamilton. We'd like to have Dr. Hayes take a look. There's video of someone talking to Hamilton, but it's grainy. There's another shot, far better, of a face that looks like the man she described. But we need to be sure."

"What about the night she was pushed?"

Kev sighed. "Too many people on that part of the platform. There's a disturbance, but it's hard to see. Probably when she fell."

Sam frowned, his gut churning hard. Whoever'd pushed her had been smart about it. "Okay. Want me to bring her to HQ?"

"That's a negative. Richie's bringing the video out."

Sam was getting used to thinking of his teammates by their call signs. Even the team captain. "We'll be here. I think shuffleboard starts in an hour, so maybe in between activities we'll find some time for videos."

Big Mac laughed. "Damn, man, you're gonna fit in with us just fine. Call if you need anything."

"Copy," Sam said, smiling in spite of himself. He liked being HOT. Being a part of Strike Team 1. He only hoped they were as good as they were supposed to be.

If not, Georgie's life was forfeit. And that was something he couldn't let happen. With everything he had in him, he would fight for her—even if he had to risk his own life in the process.

Sam glanced into the house and saw her holding her cat, talking as the animal swished her tail back and forth happily. He started to go inside, but his phone rang again. Sam bit back a groan as Rick's name popped up on his screen.

Damn, this was about to get interesting.

Chapter Fourteen

WHEN SAM CAME BACK INSIDE, HIS EXPRESSION WAS quietly grim. Georgie's heart turned over.

"What's happened?"

He only stared at her. "Rick just called me."

Georgie sighed. Dammit. "Rick needs to mind his own business."

Sam scraped a hand over his head. "You told him you'd found a boyfriend and he could stop worrying about you. That you were having the best sex of your life and Tim was a pimple on the ass of humanity."

Georgie only felt a mild sense of embarrassment at having her words repeated back to her. She stroked Belle's soft fur and sighed. "I didn't want him to worry. And the sex was pretty good, but don't let it go to your head that I said that. It was a slight exaggeration for effect."

It wasn't, but he didn't need to know that.

He looked murderous. "Jesus, Georgie. You just don't

get it, do you? Your family is convinced you're a princess and only the best will do. Not only that, but they're also worried about their princess and this new man in her life when the old one was clearly so bad for her."

Annoyance flared to life inside her. "Why do you care? I didn't say a word about you." She spread her hand to encompass the cottage. "Or about this. I said I met someone and the sex was great. I wanted Rick to get off my back, okay?"

"Yeah, but guess who wants me to check out this new boyfriend of yours?"

Georgie sighed. "So check him out and give Rick a glowing report. What's the problem?"

Sam stood there with his fists clenched at his sides, his naked chest rippling with tattooed muscle, and a fierce expression on his face. Her core flooded with heat. Oh wow he was hot.

"The problem is that I have to lie. I'm expected to investigate the guy you're sleeping with… who just so happens to be me."

Georgie put Belle down and went to him. She tilted her head back to meet his dark, glittering gaze. And then she put her hand on his pectoral, smoothing it down his abdomen and over the ridges of hard muscle. Her core was already wet.

"You aren't Rick's lackey, Sam. You have a job to do. Tell him you don't have time and tell him I'm a grown woman. It's as simple as that."

"Simple?"

She was gratified to hear his voice had dropped a

few notches. Oh how she felt those sensual tones deep in the heart of her.

"I'm not wearing any panties," she whispered. "Doesn't that make it all better?"

"Georgie," he groaned. "You're killing me here."

She reached for his belt buckle. "Oooh, you feel that? The wind is blowing. Blowing my dress right off. Blowing you right where I want you."

For a minute she thought he was going to resist her, thought he would set her away and lecture her about her choices. But he didn't. Instead, he gathered her dress in his fists and lifted it over her head.

"You really *aren't* wearing panties."

"Of course not. I wanted to be ready."

He frowned as his fingers lightly touched the bruised skin of her hip. "I'd like to maim whoever did this to you."

"Forget about them. Take care of me. I need you. Can't you tell?"

He caressed her hot, wet mound, and she thrilled at the sound of satisfaction he made as her skin burned where he touched. She gasped when his finger ghosted over her clit.

"You're naughty, G. I had no idea."

She laughed softly. "I know you won't believe this, Sam—but I didn't know it either." She looped her arms around his neck and pulled herself closer to him. "You make me that way."

His teeth flashed white in his handsome face. "You're a pretty hot mess yourself, you know that? And I fucking love it."

He captured her lips, kissing her so deeply and passionately that she melted against him, clinging to him like she had not one ounce of strength left in her body.

His hands roamed over her form, grabbed her ass, and lifted her up so her head was higher than his. She tried to put her legs around him, but he stopped her, held her high with his arms wrapped beneath her bottom. He carried her like that to the nearest surface—the couch—and then sat her on the back of it. She opened her legs as he dropped to his knees in front of her.

And then he spread her open with his fingers and curled his tongue around her clit until her nipples were tight, aching points and her body was on the edge of explosion. But he didn't let her finish that way.

Instead, when she was right there, right on the edge of bliss, he stood.

"Sam, I'm going to kill you," she gasped.

He unzipped his jeans and freed his cock. "Yeah, no doubt about it, babe. You're already killing me."

He was so hard and beautiful that she wanted to take him in her mouth and feel him pulsing against her tongue. Instead, he sheathed himself in a condom that he produced from somewhere—and then he plunged inside her.

Georgie flew apart instantly, her body rippling with her orgasm, a raw scream issuing from her throat as Sam pumped into her harder, drawing out her release in ways she'd never known were possible.

How did he do this to her? How did he know right

where to touch her? How did he know what she needed before she did?

With Tim, sex had been pretty good—sometimes even damn good. But it did not feel like this—like her entire body was on fire with sensation, like she would die if she didn't have him inside her, stroking hard into her.

She didn't need Tim like she needed her next breath.

But she did need Sam that way. *Oh God.*

She tried to reason with herself. How could she need him when he'd only just come into her life again? How could she possibly think she needed him? She needed *this*. This thing he did to her. She did not need *him*.

This kind of thing was possible with another lover. Of course it was. Surely she'd had it with Tim too and she just couldn't remember it.

And yet, as Sam lifted her legs and wrapped them around his torso, she shuddered with the thought of any other man doing this to her. It *wasn't* possible.

Because there was no other man in the world for her but this one.

There never had been.

Chapter Fifteen

"Is this the guy?" Richie sat at the small table in the kitchen and slid an 8x10 picture toward Georgie. Sam watched her reach for it with trembling fingers, and a wave of protectiveness washed through him. It was so strong he wanted to wrap her up in his embrace and never let her go.

She'd twisted him up inside but good. It was only a couple of hours ago that he'd been standing between her legs, buried deep inside her, the top of his head ready to come right off it felt so damn good. He wanted that again.

And then he wanted her to go back to Texas. He wanted her where she belonged, safe with her family, and he wanted her to find another guy to drive crazy with her hot body and wicked tongue.

He wanted a clear conscience again, but he knew he wasn't going to get it anytime soon. Yeah, he didn't really have to tell Rick anything—but he hated lying to his best friend. Rick only wanted what was best for Georgie, and while he knew she was an adult, he'd sounded pretty damn suspicious about the new man in her life.

"I don't want her hurt, Sam. Just check this guy out if you can, okay? Put the fear of God in him, same as always."

Same as always. Yeah, they'd been hell on the guys Georgie had started to "date" when she was fourteen. Oh, she hadn't been allowed to go on actual dates that early, but there'd been mall meets and football games and picnics where she'd pair off with some teenaged Romeo. And Rick and Sam were right there, frowning and wagging hypocritical fingers since they were also doing their damnedest to corrupt the teenage daughters of Hopeful's citizenry.

"That's him," Georgie said. She glanced up at Sam. He wanted to reach for her, but he didn't. Richie's gaze bounced between the two of them for a moment. The dude wasn't stupid and there were definitely undercurrents in the room.

"All right. That helps. Thanks, Dr. Hayes."

He started to stand, but Georgie reached out and caught his arm. "I want to know who those people are."

She sounded fierce now, and Sam felt a swell of pride. And annoyance since the less she knew the better.

Richie glanced at Sam as he sat back down. There were too many things she couldn't know, but there were also things they were going to have to tell her if this mission went down the way they were planning. Georgie withdrew her hand and tucked it into her lap.

"I can't tell you much," he began. "But this guy is known to associate with certain—elements, let's say—that are wanted by the US government."

"And this is why the military is involved instead of the cops?"

"Yes."

"Can you catch him?"

"We intend to. He hasn't left the country, so we'll get him."

"I don't know who *we* are. How do I know you can manage this at all?"

Richie grinned. "We specialize in this kind of thing, Dr. Hayes. And though I can't tell you specifically who *we* are, believe me when I tell you this is all part of the daily routine for us. We'll get him."

Georgie looked annoyed. "Fine. But don't we have watch lists? How did this guy get into the US anyway?"

"Unfortunately, he's a citizen. And yes, we have watch lists. Sometimes that's what we do—we just watch."

"Watching didn't help Jake Hamilton one bit." Her tone was sharp and Sam winced. Just what he needed—Georgie pissing off his CO.

Richie's gray eyes snapped with meaning. "Sergeant Hamilton had a choice. He made the wrong one."

Georgie seemed to deflate a little. "I know that, but I'm still sorry it cost him his life."

Richie squeezed her shoulder, and Sam had a crazy impulse to stop him from touching her for even a second.

"I've been doing this job a long time and I can tell

you that it never gets easier to accept death. You get immune to it in some ways, but even that comes with a price. I'm sorry it cost him his life, even if I'm not surprised."

Georgie bowed her head. "So what now? How long do I have to stay here?"

Sam tried not to read more into that question than necessary. It was normal she'd want to go back to her life.

"I'm afraid we don't know. But you're in good hands with Sergeant McKnight, so don't worry. We'll have more information in a day or two and he'll update you then."

Richie stood and Georgie brought her knees up, hugged them while she turned to look outside. Her cat jumped up on the table and head-butted her. She scratched the cat absently.

"McKnight." Richie jerked his head toward the door and Sam went with him. They walked outside and into the front yard. There was a driveway lined with trees that led out to a road about half a mile away. They were definitely remote.

Richie turned. "It's not my place to tell you how to conduct your personal affairs, but try not to let the lovely charms of Dr. Hayes cloud your judgment, okay?"

Sam stiffened. "Keeping her safe is my priority. It always has been."

Richie studied him. "Yeah, I can see that, *mon ami*," he said, his Cajun accent coming out like it did every so often. He took an envelope out of his pocket and handed it to Sam. "When I give you the signal, gonna need the professor to make the call."

"So the plan to have her set up a meeting is still the one we're going with?"

He hated that plan. Passionately. It involved Georgie too deeply.

"It's the best one we have. The FBI is watching the house in Greenbelt where they're living, but they haven't done anything yet to get themselves caught. We can't actually tie Al-Fayed to Hamilton's death. He was stabbed, but we have no weapon. Getting Al-Fayed to attempt to buy Hamilton's information is the best shot we've got."

"I don't want to put her in danger. She's not an operator."

"I know. But we'll be here. HOT won't let anything happen to her. Unfortunately, we need these guys to come after her if we're going to get them. The basic script is in the envelope along with a mockup SD card for her to sell, so get her to familiarize herself with the details of the operation. Once I give the signal, have her make the call. Those guys will come, and we'll scoop them up."

Sam's heart was pounding. "How can you be sure? What if they don't come? What if they decide to lie in wait somewhere for her? She'll never be safe if that happens."

"They're desperate. Hamilton only gave them partial information and they need the rest of it. We've been listening to the chatter. Ibn-Rashad is getting pretty nasty. If they think Dr. Hayes has what they need, they'll come for her. We'll be here when they do."

Sam hated Jake Hamilton with a vengeance right now. "Did he have the full plans or was he just scamming these guys for money?"

"If he had them, they weren't in his apartment. Al-Fayed and his associates swept the place pretty thoroughly. We've checked too." Richie shrugged. "In short, I don't know. Maybe he realized he could get more money out of them and he stashed the plans elsewhere for safekeeping. Or he hadn't managed to lift everything yet and he was buying time."

Sam folded the envelope in half and stuck it in his jeans pocket. How the fuck was he supposed to put Georgie in danger when he'd promised he never would? "I hate involving her. If Hamilton was still alive, I'd kill the guy myself for getting her into this."

Richie's's expression was both sympathetic and determined. "I know what you're feeling. That sense of helplessness while you watch the woman you love do something insanely risky—but you have to trust it will be okay. She's strong enough to do this. And you're strong enough to stand there when she does. Evie proves it to me every day, believe me. Sometimes all you can do is hold on for the ride."

Sam had heard about Richie's adventures down in Louisiana. There'd been organized crime, car chases, explosions, and a missing teenager, among other things. And though he'd gone down there single, he'd come back with a sexy chef who now wore a pretty spectacular engagement ring. Sam had met her, and while she was smoking hot, what he really adored was the food she'd sent into HOT HQ with Richie recently.

Damn, that girl could cook.

Richie turned and got into his car while Sam stood there, hands shoved in pockets, and brooded. He couldn't stop thinking about one word the man had used —love. What the fuck was that supposed to mean?

Of course he loved Georgie. He'd loved her since they were kids. But it wasn't *that* kind of love. How could it be? They'd only started having sex last night. Before that, they hadn't seen each other in six years. How on earth could romantic love be a part of the equation? And how could someone who didn't know either one of them all that well think it was?

Sam went back into the house after Richie's car disappeared from sight and found Georgie in the same position as when he'd left. Her eyes, when she turned to look at him, were troubled.

"This isn't going to end easily, is it?"

He wasn't sure what she was talking about. The situation with the Freedom Force—God, that was a fucking joke of a name, wasn't it?—or this thing between them. That's how twisted up she had him. He didn't even know what they were talking about.

She put her knees down and ran her hands through her gorgeous mane of hair—which had been hanging free since he'd unclipped it earlier.

"Fucking terrorist assholes," she spat. "And fucking Jake Hamilton for being greedy or idealistic or whatever in the fuck he was being. He was an overachiever, and he liked nothing more than to get a perfect score. Bet it was the same thing with this DARPA shit. He wanted to do it because he liked the game, nothing else."

"I'm sorry, G. I know you liked him."

"I did. And I'm pissed as hell he did something so stupid."

"Some people are impatient. Or they don't think they're capable of getting what they want the regular way. Who knows what kind of background he had? He might have been poor or abused or any number of things that made him long to be something better in life."

Her eyes glittered with tears. "You were poor. Your parents mentally abused you. And the last thing you would ever do is try to sell government secrets to terrorists."

"That's true. On all accounts." He didn't like admitting what his childhood had been like, but Georgie already knew. She was one of the few who did.

She looked fierce all of a sudden. "You're a good guy, Sam. An amazing guy. I want to see you after this, and I don't care if my family knows. You make me feel good about myself. Not that I don't generally feel good or anything, but getting dumped knocked the wind out of me for a while. You make me remember what I felt like before any of that happened."

He swallowed, hard. "That might be the nicest thing anyone's ever said to me. But you know it can't last, G. We're too different. I don't fit into your world—"

She swore so colorfully that he lost his train of

thought. "What world? The one where I take the Metro to the Pentagon and teach college classes to military students? Or the one where all I can think about is having you inside me? Or maybe the one where I go to bed every night with a book and Belle and feel sorry for myself because my husband didn't find me interesting enough in the long run?"

"I already told you Tim was a fucking asshole," he growled. "But dammit, you know what I mean. You're Junior League, country club, everything I'm not. Hell, I don't even know the right word half the time and you teach the right words on a daily basis. I can conjugate fuck pretty well—but that's about it. I'm a soldier, Georgie. It's as simple as that."

Her eyes glittered. "I don't care, Sam. That's the part you don't get. I don't *care* what you think your place in my life is. I know where I want you, and you won't convince me otherwise." She pointed a finger at him. "And FYI, genius, but being a soldier is pretty damned awesome. Anyone who doesn't respect your accomplishments is stupid and not worthy of your time."

Now he was pissed. Because she wasn't listening and there was no way she was truly prepared for what his life as a Special Operator entailed. "Do you really want to be a part of this kind of life? The kind where I disappear for weeks on end? Where I can't call you and can't let you know that I'm even alive?"

She swallowed but didn't say anything, and he knew he'd made a point she couldn't refute. But he still kept going.

"Christ, Georgie, you freaked out because a student

went missing from your class. What the hell will you do when it's me who's missing? Call my fucking boss and demand to know where I am? Do you really think that'll work?"

Her eyes filled with tears and his heart ripped in two. He didn't stay to see if they would fall.

Chapter Sixteen

Georgie watched Sam walk out of the house and into the yard. She wanted to call him back, wanted to say she was sorry, but he'd pretty much stunned her. And he was right. How could she stomach the life he led after she'd felt so out of control of her own life these past couple of years?

Tim had abandoned her for another woman. Jake Hamilton skipped class a few times and she'd gone looking for him. What would she do when it was Sam who left? How could she possibly have a life with him when he was right that she wouldn't like it?

And why did she even think she wanted that life? She'd had a crush on him once and they'd had sex. So what? That wasn't a recipe for the future, no matter that he made her feel good about herself again for the first time in a long time.

Georgie swiped her fingers under her eyes and wiped the moisture on her clothing. And then she grabbed her computer, determined to get some work done. Eventually, Sam came back inside. She didn't know what to say so she didn't say anything. He walked over to her side and thrust a piece of paper at her.

"What's this?"

Sam looked grim. "You're going to have to make a call sometime in the next couple of days. Everything you need to know about it is on this paper along with a basic script. It's best if you practice so you can sound natural."

She read the first few words, her blood going cold. "I'm supposed to tell them I have the information. And that I'll sell it for a hundred thousand dollars in cash? Oh my God."

Sam shrugged. "Yeah."

She read the paper over a few times. "Drone technology? That's what Jake was selling them?"

"Yes."

"What the hell was he thinking?"

"He was probably thinking it didn't matter because it wouldn't affect him."

She cocked her head. This was already more information than she'd expected they'd tell her about what Jake had been doing. But if she was going to sell the idea she had something these people wanted, she had to know what it was.

"What do you mean it wouldn't affect him?"

"He wasn't deployable. If somebody weaponized the technology and used it against our deployed soldiers, it wasn't going to affect him. He'd be here."

Anger throbbed in her belly. "That's disgusting. And immoral."

"Yes."

She looked down at the words again. They blurred a little, but it was anger rather than tears that made it happen. "I'll get it right."

"I know you will. And Georgie, you realize you can't talk about any of this once it's over, right?"

Her gaze snapped to his. "Of course I do! I'm not an idiot. I also care about the soldiers I teach, so I don't want any of them in danger. *Ever*."

They were in jeopardy because of their jobs sometimes, but damned if she'd be the cause of any additional peril.

The lines around his eyes softened. "I know you care, G. You need to read the words aloud. Really get them in your head and mouth."

"Is this the kind of thing you do all the time?"

Sam was standing over her, hands in pockets, frowning. He hadn't said a word about earlier, but they both knew it was still there between them. "It's part of it."

She shook her head, the enormity of what he did pressing into her brain. "When you left to join the Army, I don't think I pictured this. I pictured tanks and guns. And believe me, I didn't like the idea of that at all. But this seems more frightening somehow."

"That's what I've been trying to tell you." He sucked in a breath, blew it out again. "I did the other stuff for a while. This is something new, and yeah, it's dangerous. But it's important, Georgie. What we do—the guys I work with, me—keeps this country safe."

She'd always thought of the Army as dangerous and she'd hated that he might be in jeopardy. But *this*.

This secret organization—because she had no doubt that's what it was—was simply another layer to an already risky career.

"Are you happy with your choices?"

His jaw flexed. "Yes." He let out a sigh and sat down across from her. "This job is me. It's something I'm good at. If I'd stayed in Hopeful, I'd have never amounted to much. Even with your family's influence. I couldn't afford college, and without it there were no jobs I'd ever grow with. I didn't want the mill, Georgie."

"You could have gotten student loans, could have worked for my dad—"

"No." His voice was a whip in the air between them. "That's what you don't understand. What none of you understand. I'm not helpless and I'm not a charity case. Besides, I like what I do. It makes me damn proud to say I rescue people and stop terrorists, because not everyone can do it. But I can, Georgie. Me, fucked-up Sam McKnight."

Her heart filled. Sam was driven to succeed and he'd done it on his own terms. He was still doing it. How could she fault him for that? She'd left Hopeful too and she didn't much appreciate her family trying to pull her back. "I understand."

His eyes said he didn't believe it. "Do you? Or are you just saying that?"

"I'm trying." She reached for his hand and squeezed it. "Yes, I care about you, and yes, it worries me that you're in danger. I'd be worried if you were a policeman or a fireman too. And you aren't fucked up. Or at least no more than the rest of us are."

"It's nice of you to say that."

She laughed. It wanted to turn into a sob but she wouldn't let it. "I'm not being nice. Trust me, I know fucked up. Just because someone seems to have a perfect life on the outside doesn't mean they do. My husband cheated on me, lied to me, and left me for another woman. I'd say that's pretty fucked up."

Sam sighed and scrubbed a hand over his head. "Yeah, all right, you got me there. We can both be fucked up then." He nudged his chin at the paper in her hand. "Now how about you read that a few times and let's see how it sounds."

She skimmed the words again, her belly twisting. "Does this mean I have to actually meet with them? That they'll come here?"

He nodded, though he didn't look happy about it. "I'll be with you. My guys will be outside, surrounding us. You won't be in danger. Get the conversation down in your head first, then we'll go over what happens if they agree to meet here."

Georgie nibbled her lip. She thought of Jake Hamilton, of Sam, of Matt Girard—and of the other men she'd met in the military facility he'd taken her to. So serious and dedicated. Unlike Jake, who'd only been looking for a way to enrich himself.

And crushing on her, apparently. The thought made her shudder.

"I won't let you down, Sam," she said firmly. She wouldn't let any of them down. She couldn't. Not when she knew what they risked to keep the world safe.

"I know you won't."

His words made her feel good, and yet worry still clung to her like a second skin.

She shoved it down deep and focused on the paper.

She'd get this right. For all of them.

Chapter Seventeen

Georgie memorized the details of the operation and practiced saying what she needed to tell Jake's murderer while Sam went out into the yard to engage in some kind of workout routine that left her breathless.

He was wearing athletic shorts, nothing else, and breathing deeply while moving through a set of exercises that left his body dripping with sweat.

Georgie tried not to ache deep inside, but that was about as fruitless as trying to prevent a dog from eating a plate of bacon left on the floor. She worked a bit, grading the papers she had left, and looking over the final exam one more time. It was two days before it had to be administered and she held out a crazy hope this might all be over by then and she'd go back to her usual routine.

Well, except for one thing.

She still wanted Sam as a part of her routine. She didn't know how that would happen, especially since he'd pointed out the obvious conflict between his life and hers.

Yes, she had freaked out when her student went missing. And yeah, she'd had half a marriage with Tim for the last couple of years and she wasn't precisely ready to engage in the kind of relationship where she had no idea where her man was or what he was doing.

How would she handle that?

She'd felt a vague uneasiness over Tim's late nights at work, but she'd told herself it was silly. He was working hard at a new job.

Except it wasn't that at all.

Because he'd been working hard all right, giving it to Lindsey until late and then coming home and showering before crashing into bed and starting the whole thing over again the next morning.

Georgie bit her lip. God, what a fool she'd been. But they'd been arguing so much then and she'd really preferred the quiet time alone when he was supposedly working. She'd read books, worked on her lesson plans, and waited for him to come home.

When weeks passed without sex, she'd felt relief rather than worry. Just when she started to believe something was wrong, Tim would make love to her and they'd have a blissful few days before everything went sideways again.

Sam was still working out, his muscles bunching and flexing, glowing with sweat. Her core clenched tight. How could she want to leap into a relationship with a man who would give her even less stability than Tim had?

She shook her head and tried to concentrate on her computer. When she read the same sentence for the twentieth time, she snapped the computer shut and propped her chin in her hands so she could watch Sam.

Eventually he came inside and she pretended to be busy while he went and took a shower. When he returned, smelling like soap and looking delicious with his hair slicked back, he quizzed her on the information she'd learned. Once he was satisfied, they fell into silence.

Georgie didn't know what to say to him, so she said nothing. Sam spent time cleaning his weapon and reporting in to his super-secret military organization every hour.

When dinnertime rolled around, they ate leftover pasta with wine. Sam even baked a chocolate cake in the microwave, which she found super impressive. She told him so and he grinned.

"Even I can read a cookbook, G."

She took another bite of the cake. It wasn't beautiful but it sure was good. "Yeah, but you don't have a cookbook here. You've memorized this, and I'm impressed. I wouldn't begin to know how to do it."

He shrugged. "You'd learn if you wanted. I like chocolate cake. And it's easier to learn how to do it yourself than buy a slice in a coffee shop."

"I don't know. I'd think the coffee shop was easier."

The look he gave her was full of meaning. "When there *is* a coffee shop. Sometimes there isn't."

He meant when he was deployed somewhere. She

finished the last bite of cake and sighed. "Well, good news for your team or squad or whatever."

His grin was genuine. "Yeah, I get stuck cooking when we have facilities."

She blinked. "And what do you do when you don't?" She didn't imagine they had takeout in some of the places he went to.

"MREs."

"Oh yes, how could I forget those?"

Meals Ready to Eat came in sealed pouches, packed about a million calories per meal, and had been known to cause some pretty desperate trips to the restroom when you weren't accustomed to eating them. Or so she'd been told.

"No one ever forgets MREs, believe me."

"So I've heard." She got up and collected his plate and took everything over to the sink. She washed the dishes quickly, and then set them in the strainer to dry. When she turned around, Sam was watching her, his expression intense and heated. Her heart skipped a beat.

"If I could be with anyone, I'd pick you," he said.

She licked suddenly dry lips. "You can. All we have to do is try."

He shook his head and her heart fell. "I already know how it'll go. Tried it once before and it didn't work out."

She didn't know why it pierced her to think of Sam having a relationship with another woman. She'd been *married*, for goodness sake. But it kicked her in the chest to think of him with anyone else.

"I'm sorry it didn't work out, Sam."

He shrugged. "It's fine. It happens."

"What if I wanted to try anyway?"

She could tell he'd stiffened where he sat. "Best not to go down that road, Georgie. I'd rather have this—these few memories of you—than know I wasn't what you wanted me to be."

She wanted to go over and shake him. "You keep saying that. But how do you know what I want you to be? What if I just want you to be yourself?"

He got to his feet and stretched and she knew he was through with this conversation. "I better check in with HQ now."

He turned to walk away, but she couldn't let him go so easily. "You know," she called, "I had the *right* man with the *right* connections—and a fat lot of good it did me. The only person who cares that you aren't part of the country club set is you, Sam."

He turned back to her, his eyes glittering. "Maybe so. But that still doesn't change the fact that what I do isn't normal. Or stable. Are you ready for that, Georgie? Can you honestly say you are?"

Her throat was tight. "I don't know. But I'd like the chance to figure it out."

He looked cool and remote, and she knew he wasn't even considering it. Then he shook his head. "I'm right, Georgie. About everything. You'll realize it eventually. And you'll be thankful you had a near miss."

She wanted to growl. "Don't tell me what I'm supposed to be feeling. I'll work that out for myself, thanks."

He only arched an eyebrow before he pulled his

phone from his pocket and walked outside. She watched him go down into the yard, away from her, and start to talk to someone on the other end. She wanted to scream. Instead, she hugged her arms around herself and wished this nightmare would soon be over. If she were in her home, her bed, her life—well, maybe she wouldn't ache so much when Sam McKnight refused to consider any kind of future where she might fit in.

When it got late, Georgie went to get ready for bed. Sam didn't even look up when she left, and she wondered how this night would go compared to last night. When she finished her nightly routine and went back out to the kitchen to grab some water, Sam was on the cot, eyes closed, arms folded over his impressive chest.

It was precisely what she expected—and yet she fumed for several minutes before she went and climbed into bed alone. Georgeanne Hayes was not begging. She'd come perilously close to it earlier when he'd told her there was no chance for them, but that was a line she wasn't going to cross—no matter how needy she felt or how much she ached for him.

But of course sleep wouldn't come as she lay there alone, knowing Sam was in the next room, knowing what kind of heat they'd already shared. She'd been in bed for an hour, maybe two, lying awake with the covers tossed back and her heart pounding in frustration, when her door opened. Sam came in on silent feet and then stripped before lowering himself onto the mattress.

She wanted desperately to turn into him, to roll her hips against his body and beg him for fulfillment—but she was angry and she couldn't do that without being weak. She didn't like being weak.

"What are you doing?" she demanded. "I thought we were finished."

He rolled her beneath him in a single smooth move and she realized he was hard. Her core flooded with heat. She barely suppressed a whimper. She should tell him to go away, but there was no way in hell she was going to do it.

No way.

"We should be, but God knows I can't get a moment's rest with you in the next room. Not when I want you so bad." He flexed his hips and her body arched up off the bed, though she willed it not to.

"Sam. My God…" Her voice choked with need.

"This is what life with me is like, Georgie. Nothing for days on end—and then there I am, in your bed, in your life, wanting you to drop everything and be with me. Because I've been out in the field and now I'm back and I need you."

Her breath was coming faster now. She could tell it tortured him to say these things, but she wanted to hear it. Wanted to understand. His life terrified her, but she needed him all the same. "I like being needed."

"And if I only need you for sex? If all I want is a hot fuck before I'm gone again?"

"Maybe that's all *I* want. Did you ever consider that?"

He stiffened and she knew that thought had never crossed his mind. Well, hell, it hadn't crossed hers either, but damn if she'd let him be the one to say those kinds of things, to make assumptions about her feelings—even if they were mostly true.

She'd always done what she'd been expected to do. She'd married the proper guy and followed him around while he advanced in his career—and look how that had worked out for her. Maybe it was time she did something shocking. Maybe it was time she threw herself into a sexual relationship with a man and worked out the details as they happened.

Except, God, she really didn't see herself operating that way. Not when the man was Sam and she'd loved him for half her life.

His mouth dropped to the column of her throat and she sighed as his lips and tongue left a trail of flame in their wake. There was *nothing* better than this feeling she got when he was making love to her.

Sam McKnight was her drug of choice, and she needed her fix.

Regardless that the fall to the bottom of the pit would be damn hard when it came.

"Georgie, you have to start thinking about this. You can't want me beyond these few days. I'm good for nothing but this kind of thing. I can't give you what you deserve."

She lifted her head and nipped his earlobe. "I'll be the judge of what I deserve." She wrapped her legs around his waist, held on tight. "Go ahead, Sam. Do what you think is your absolute worst. I need it. I need *you*."

He rocked into her body with a single sharp thrust and she gasped with the intensity of the pleasure he gave her. Everything felt so right when she was with Sam. So gloriously good.

He began to thrust into her hard, deep, and sure, until she was a mass of raw nerve endings, until the explosion took hold of her and magnified her senses to a keen edge. He followed her, her name a broken groan on his lips. And then he gathered her close and she remembered nothing else as she fell into a deep sleep.

Chapter Eighteen

GEORGIE WASN'T QUITE SURE, BUT SHE THOUGHT THAT Sam decided to stop fighting with her about the future. Or at least that he'd determined not to think about it. Because for the next two days, he was with her every moment. They spent hours in bed together, learning the taste and texture of each other, and they spent hours talking. About anything and everything—except for the specifics of his job in the military. She knew that part was off-limits, and she understood why.

But they did talk about the things he'd done, the places he'd gone. She learned the number and position of his scars, his calluses, the first time he'd shot a man, and the first time he'd been shot.

She ached for him, and she wanted to hold him tight and never let him go. Not that he would let her. If he had any idea how protective she felt, how angry she grew when she thought of him wounded and laid up in a hospital with no one to visit him except his Army buddies, then perhaps he wouldn't tell her these things.

And that she could not bear. So she kept silent and she listened. And then she told him things about herself.

Sam wanted to know about her relationship with Tim, and she found herself saying what she'd never told anyone else. Sam listened attentively, but he frowned a lot.

"He didn't deserve you, Georgie," he finally said.

Georgie felt a flood of warmth deep inside. "I know." And then she reached for his hand. "I know exactly what I deserve now."

He'd stopped protesting when she said things like that, but she didn't kid herself he'd made his peace with it. He still watched her with those wary eyes when he thought she didn't know it. She knew he was turning it over in his head, thinking about his job, about Rick and her parents, and about everything he thought he couldn't give her.

Of course she knew what her family wanted for her. They'd always wanted her coddled and privileged, wanted her to be with a man who didn't want her for the money in her trust fund.

Sam didn't want her trust fund, but he was certain her family would think he did. And he was too proud to endure that. She knew he didn't want handouts. From anyone. It tortured him to think her family might think less of him. She understood now that a great part of why he'd worked so hard to make something of himself was to prove that he could. To prove that her parents' faith in him hadn't been misplaced.

It touched her and broke her heart all at once. And

she couldn't convince him it didn't matter because to him it did.

His phone rang early on the fourth evening of their time together. Every time he got a call she held her breath, but so far it hadn't been the call he'd been waiting for—the one that said it was time for her to call the terrorists.

But this time was different. She could tell by the tension evident in every line of his body.

When Sam hung up, he stared at her for a long moment. "You ready for this, babe?"

Her belly churned with fear. "Yes."

"The FBI has been watching the cell, and there's surveillance video that places Abdullah al-Fayed—that's the guy you saw—close to the spot where Hamilton's body was found. That's not enough to convict him though. We need more."

"So I have to arrange a meeting to sell the information." She blew out a breath. "I can do it, Sam. I'm ready."

His expression was troubled. "I hate that you're involved. I feel like I'm betraying your whole family to put you in danger this way."

Something hot and sweet flowed through her. "Sam." She got up and went to his side. He dragged her down into his lap and wrapped his arms around her. She lay her head against his. "You'll protect me. You and your guys. You said so, and I believe you."

He squeezed her a little tighter. "I'll protect you with my life, Georgie."

Her heart hitched. "I don't want *that*. Just protect

me. Shoot those bastards if you have to, but don't you dare sacrifice yourself for some bizarre reason."

He laughed softly, his body shaking beneath her. "Believe me, I'm not about to sacrifice myself. I'm not that helpless. But if I *had* to die to keep you safe, I would. Just so you know."

She put her hands on either side of his face. Cupped him almost fiercely. "Don't say stuff like that."

His eyes searched hers. "Okay."

"Kiss me, Sam. Please."

His grip tightened. "There's no time."

"There's always time. You can make me come in three seconds. You know that."

He laughed. "I suppose we can spare three seconds."

"Damn straight we can."

Sam kissed her and the world faded away.

———

"YOU CAN DO THIS, BABY," Sam said as Georgie held her phone and took deep breaths. They'd spent a little longer than three seconds making each other feel good, but it was over now and there was nothing left to do except call Abdullah al-Fayed at the number Richie had given them.

"I know." Georgie's mouth was red, her lips luscious and swollen from the force of his kisses. His body still zinged with sparks. He was pretty sure hers did too. Her nipples were tight little points in her T-shirt and he ached to spend more time touching them.

Like he hadn't spent the past four days touching

them—licking, sucking, biting—and coming on them one memorable time.

"Once we set up the exchange, that's it. We'll get those bastards and you'll be safe."

Except he didn't want her to do it. At all. It terrified him to think of Georgie having anything to do with capturing a terrorist. But they had no choice. Jake Hamilton was the common denominator. Al-Fayed wouldn't trust anyone else who happened to show up for negotiations. It had to be Georgie because he believed she'd been Jake's girlfriend.

Georgie punched in the number, her phone on speaker. Someone answered on the first ring. "Dr. Hayes," he said, and Sam's gut tightened at Al-Fayed's use of her name.

Georgie's brows drew down. "How did you know it was me?"

"Because only Jake Hamilton called me at this number."

"Oh."

"Are you alone, Dr. Hayes?"

Georgie looked guilt-stricken. She was too honest for this kind of thing. She frowned harder. "I am at the moment."

"Take your phone off speaker."

"I'm fixing dinner. It's easier this way."

"Nevertheless, you will take your phone off speaker or this call is over."

Georgie stabbed at her phone's screen and then lifted it to her ear. "Fine. I'm off speaker. Geez, paranoid much?"

A small part of Sam was laughing at her for saying it. The rest of him was on edge.

"Yes, well, I know what you said about contacting me, but I needed to think. And I think I have what you want. Maybe we could make an arrangement." She paused for a long moment while Al-Fayed spoke. "It's an SD card he gave me for safe keeping. The plans for the DARPA long-range drone project are on here. Jake said if he didn't come back, I should destroy it. But I'd rather have the money. You *were* planning to pay him for this stuff, right? One hundred thousand dollars in cash?"

She sounded so mercenary. So calm and cool. He watched her intently, proud of her, amazed by her—and terrified for her at the same time.

"Yes, we can meet. I'm staying on the Eastern Shore. I'll give you the address." She paused again. "You don't want to come to me? Seriously? I thought you wanted this stuff."

Sam nodded.

"Well of course I won't be alone. I'm staying with a friend. You come out here, bring a friend if you like, and we'll make an exchange. My friend will make sure you don't try to kill me like you killed Jake, you'll give me the cash, I'll give you the card, and then you can go."

Georgie met his gaze. He waited while Al-Fayed talked to her.

"Look, I don't care if you get this thing or not—if you don't want to come out here, then forget it. I can find another buyer. I'd rather be done with it than have to find someone else, but I'm not stupid and I'm not putting myself in danger. You already tried to push me off a train platform. You're lucky I'm even talking to you after that."

That last part wasn't in the script, but it was a good touch. He gave her a thumbs up. She'd learned well.

Georgie grinned suddenly, nodding. "Okay, fine. I'll text you the address. You bring your friend and I'll have mine. You can verify the info is intact, give me money, and we'll be done. Easy peasy, right?"

A second later, Georgie lowered the phone and tapped the button to end the call. Her hands were trembling. "Wow."

Sam cupped her cheek. "Perfect, baby. Absolutely perfect."

"I had to wing it a little bit at the end. He didn't want to come out here at all."

He took her phone and texted their address to the number she'd just called. "Of course he didn't. He expects a trap."

She arched an eyebrow as he handed it back. "Well he's not wrong, is he?"

"No, he's not wrong. But we don't want to do this in a public place. He doesn't either. He was just hoping you were inexperienced enough to go where he wanted you to go."

"The SD card… it's not really filled with Top Secret information, is it?"

"No. It's a mockup that my guys made. Al-Fayed will want to check the information, and it'll look real enough when he does—but it's not anything that would compromise national security."

"Why did they kill Jake if he was going to sell them the real information?"

"Best we can figure, Jake only gave Al-Fayed part of the information at their last meeting. He was probably trying to get more money. But something went wrong and Al-Fayed killed him."

"And now he believes I have the plans."

Sam nodded. "Jake must have suggested you did at some point."

Georgie frowned. "He really didn't care about anybody but himself did he?"

"Doesn't seem like it, no."

Georgie pushed her hair over her shoulder. "I feel like a shitty judge of character right now. I liked him."

He knew she was thinking about her ex-husband as well as Jake Hamilton. But neither of them was her fault. Georgie was the kind of person who took others at face value. And both men had presented her with the faces they'd wanted her to see.

"People can be shitty and they can smile in your face and hide their true nature from you. Don't blame yourself."

She nodded. "I'm getting there, Sam." She pulled in a breath and gave him a serious look. "So now we wait."

"Yes." He skimmed his hands up her arms. "My guys will be in position out there. Al-Fayed won't hurt you. I won't let it happen."

"I know you won't. I'm not wrong about your character. I may not be a good judge of other people, but I know *you* down to your soul, Sam McKnight. There's nobody I trust more."

He pulled her against him and hugged her tight.
He hoped like hell she still trusted him tomorrow.

Chapter Nineteen

Georgie paced nervously. Sam sat calmly at the table and checked his weapons. He'd tucked three pistols away on his body and just as many knives. Her pulse throbbed in her neck as her heart pumped blood faster than usual.

"Baby, it's okay," Sam told her. "We're surrounded by Special Operators and I'm right here with you."

She stopped. "Special Operator? Isn't that like Delta Force or something?"

He shot her a grin. "Something." He rose to his full height, all six feet two inches of him, and came over to squeeze her shoulders. "They're out there, Georgie. Waiting."

"How do you know? What if they got held up in traffic?"

He touched a hand to his ear. "I can hear them, that's how. And they can hear me."

Her eyebrows shot up. Had they been listening when—?

Sam smiled and shook his head, accurately reading her expression. "They've been in place since I got the phone call an hour ago. Remember that?"

"Oh. Yes."

She'd been trying to read *As I Lay Dying* for class next semester and failing miserably. She hated that particular Faulkner story with a passion, which was why she hadn't been paying attention to what Sam was doing at the time.

"It'll be any minute now," he said. "Are you ready?"

Her stomach twisted. "As ready as I'll ever be."

"When Al-Fayed and his friend get here, I'll let them in. You sit at the table like we discussed. One of them will want to check the card with a computer. They'll bring their own. Let them have it and don't say anything you don't have to."

"I know, Sam. You already told me everything."

"Just making sure. It should go pretty fast. He'll verify the card, I'll verify the money, and they'll walk out. My team will pick them up outside and it'll be over."

"I just wish they'd get here. I want this to be done. Well, this part of it anyway," she added. She hoped Sam understood her. She didn't want what they had to be over. Not yet. Hell, maybe not ever, which was a frightening prospect considering the ugliness of her last relationship.

Except she knew Sam wouldn't do that to her. If he didn't want her, he'd tell her honestly, not pretend he cared while screwing someone else.

The thought of him with anyone else made hot jealousy flare.

"Copy that, Big Mac," Sam said, turning away from her as he drew a black pistol from the holster at his waist. "We're ready. Over and out."

Georgie sucked in a breath, blew it out again. "They're coming?"

"Yes. Go sit at the table."

"Okay." She started for the table where her computer sat. Beside it was the SD card. She spun back to where Sam was standing by the door, waiting so calmly for the knock that would come. "Did you lock Belle in the bedroom?" she asked in a panic.

Sam smiled at her. "Yes, G. She was lying on the pillows when I closed the door."

"You told me that already, didn't you?" She smoothed a hand nervously over her stomach.

"I did. Now sit down, honey. Let's do this like we talked about, okay? You don't have to do a thing except give them the card. I'll be with you the whole way."

Georgie nodded as she sank onto the chair at the dining table. "I'll be fine. I won't screw this up."

"I know you won't."

The walls seemed to be made of paper now. She could hear everything outside—the frogs in the marshes, the calls of night birds, and the crunch of tires on gravel as a car made its way closer.

Doors slammed. Her heart raced. Her palms sweated.

Sam stood by the door, his attention laser-focused. And then the knock they'd been expecting came. Sam had a pistol in his hand as he grabbed the knob and swung the door wide.

Two men stood in the entry, both holding weapons. Georgie gasped, but Sam was prepared. He'd been standing beside the door, not in front of it, and he calmly leveled the pistol at the head of the first guy.

"Eject the magazines and put 'em down, boys," he ordered.

Georgie recognized the man from the Metro who'd been talking to Jake that night. The other man was the one who'd threatened her in the coffee shop.

"No deal," Metro Man said. "We aren't going unarmed while you have a weapon."

"You want the SD card or not?"

"How do we know you won't kill us and take the money?"

Sam grinned. "You don't. But it's a lot messier that way and I'd rather not have to clean up the bodies. No alligators in the marsh or I'd be tempted, I gotta tell you."

The two men exchanged a look. Metro Man looked furious as he ejected his magazine and tucked it into his pants. He placed the gun on the table by the door. Coffee Shop Man did the same, shrugging as if to say *who cares?*

Coffee Shop Man had a messenger bag slung over his chest. Sam motioned to it. "Let's see inside the bag."

Coffee Shop Man unclipped the flap and jerked it back. Then he held it open.

"There is one hundred thousand dollars, like we promised. And my computer," Metro Man said.

Georgie assumed he was Abdullah al-Fayed since he appeared to be the one in control.

Sam peered inside. "I'm going to have to count that money."

"And I'm going to have to verify the contents of the SD card. Where is it?"

Sam nodded toward her. "Dr. Hayes has it."

Al-Fayed started to reach inside the bag.

"Slowly," Sam said. "Or you're gonna lose a hand."

Hatred was clearly written on Al-Fayed's face as he reached very slowly into the bag. He lifted out a silver MacBook inch by inch. "Satisfied?"

"For now."

"And may I join Dr. Hayes at the table?"

"Sure thing, Skippy. But you try anything, and I'll blow your head clean off your shoulders."

———

"THE ONE WITH the bag is Imran Nassif. The other is our boy Al-Fayed. And they didn't come alone," Richie said in his ear. "Another vehicle, six of them getting out with weapons."

Sam hated that he couldn't respond, but responding would let Al-Fayed and Nassif know that Sam and Georgie weren't alone either.

"Copy," Big Mac said. "We'll move in closer."

"Nobody make any sudden moves. We don't want them knowing we're out here before it's time," Richie replied. "We need them to pay for the drone information."

Sam didn't want Al-Fayed anywhere near Georgie, but if that's how the bosses said it had to go down, then that's how it had to go down. But damn if he didn't hate every agonizing second of it.

Al-Fayed had stiffened at Sam's dismissive comment, his nostrils flaring wide. The man didn't like being in a position where he had no power. At all.

"Both of you," Sam said, jerking his pistol in the direction of Georgie. "At the table. Sparky and I can count money while you check the veracity of your info."

Al-Fayed was grinding his teeth. "Sure thing, John Wayne."

Sam grinned. "Aw, there you go, complimenting me when we hardly know each other."

They moved toward the table and Sam took a seat beside Georgie, across from where the other two men sat. Nassif placed the bag on the table, flap up. Al-Fayed popped the top of his Mac open, nostrils still flaring as he glared at them all.

"If you would be so kind, Dr. Hayes," he said.

Georgie vibrated with tension but she pulled the SD card from beneath the notebook she'd placed on top of it and pushed it at Al-Fayed. He grasped it eagerly and shoved it into the SD dongle he'd attached to the Mac.

Meanwhile, Nassif pulled ten bound stacks of crisp one hundred-dollar bills from the bag and placed them one on top of another. For a hundred K, it didn't look like much. Only about five inches high.

But that was correct. It wasn't the first time Sam had seen so much money in one place. Probably wouldn't be the last. He knew what a hundred grand looked like in hundreds. He also knew what it looked like in twenties.

"Interesting," Al-Fayed murmured as he opened the files.

Kid snorted in Sam's ear. "He's trying to send it somewhere, probably so he can tell you it's not what he wants and get out of paying for it. Damn, he must really think Dr. Hayes is an idiot."

"You're jamming that signal, right?" somebody asked. Sam thought it might be Ryan "Flash" Gordon.

"Dude, what do you take me for? Of course I'm jamming it. Nothing's getting out of here without my say so."

"The six are moving closer to the house. They've got AR-15s with night scopes. Fucking wannabes," Richie growled. "Close the perimeter on these bastards. I want them taken down the minute those fuckers come out of the house."

Tension knotted Sam's gut. Not that he typically cared about terrorists bearing down on his position when he had his team at his back, but he didn't usually have the woman he loved at his side either.

Everything inside him went still. *Love?* He loved Georgie Hayes?

Yes, came the answer. *Hell yes.*

He wanted to look at her so badly, but he couldn't do it. Couldn't let these bastards see that she was his vulnerability. If they had any clue at all, they might use his feelings against him.

Feelings.

Holy shit, he was so fucked. He loved her, probably

always had, and she wasn't his. Could never be his, no matter what she thought. She wasn't made for his kind of life. The fact she vibrated with nerves beside him confirmed it.

Fresh fear coiled inside him but he pushed it deep and refused to let it out. "Count the money," Sam told Nassif, getting back on track. "Where I can see it."

Nassif's eyes flashed but he picked up the first stack of cash and started to methodically count. Sam pretended to follow along but the truth was he didn't fucking care if there were wads of newspaper stuffed between those hundred dollar bills on either end. He just wanted this done and these guys on their way.

Al-Fayed looked up a few minutes later, his dark gaze spearing into Georgie. "If any piece of this information proves incorrect, nothing and no one will protect you. I will find you, and I will do to you what I did to Jake Hamilton."

Sam's gut twisted at the threat. But Georgie answered before he could.

"I grew up in Texas, Mr. Al-Fayed. I've shot many a rattlesnake in my life and I'm not afraid to shoot another one. You come after me and you might not survive the trip. I'm selling you what Jake gave me. If it's not what you want, then that's your problem, not mine."

Al-Fayed slapped the laptop closed and jerked his head at Nassif. "Give them the money. We're going. This meeting is over."

Sam waved his pistol at Al-Fayed. "Now hold on, Skippy. We're not quite done counting it yet."

"Then hurry up," Al-Fayed said from between clenched teeth.

Nassif counted the remaining bills faster. Sam kept an eye on Al-Fayed.

"One hundred thousand," Nassif finished.

Sam pulled a marker from his pocket. "Dr. Hayes, pull ten random bills and check for counterfeits."

He didn't fucking care, but he had to pretend he did. Otherwise they might know something was fishy about the whole setup.

Georgie uncapped the pen and selected a bill. Before she could mark it, gunfire shattered the night.

"Fuck!" somebody yelled on the comm link. "Knight Rider, get her out of there. STAT!"

Chapter Twenty

Georgie froze at the sound of gunfire. Al-Fayed and his companion leapt to their feet at the same time Sam did. He leveled the pistol at the two men, but they were surprisingly unaffected.

"Show him," Al-Fayed growled.

Coffee Shop Man ripped open his shirt, buttons flying as he did so. He grabbed something that lay against his skin. It took her a moment to realize there were wires on his chest, tape—and a timer.

"Shoot him and the bomb goes off. Shoot me and he'll detonate it," Al-Fayed said, smiling evilly. "I suggest you put the weapon down, John Wayne. And tell your people to back off."

Sam didn't drop the pistol. He also didn't pull the trigger. "I'll hold onto it, if you don't mind," he gritted out from between his teeth. "And I don't have any people."

"Then who's doing the shooting?"

"You tell me. You didn't come alone like she told

you, and whoever you brought with you is scared of the marsh at night. That wasn't targeted gunfire. That was an idiot shooting at ghosts."

Al-Fayed flushed but didn't answer. "Return the money to the bag," he said. "We'll be taking it with us."

The gunfire outside had stopped as quickly as it started. But it was eerily quiet now. Even the frogs had ceased croaking. The night sounds she'd gotten used to were gone. Georgie strained to hear anything over the quiet, but there was nothing.

Was Sam's team still out there? Or had something happened to them? Of course Al-Fayed brought people with him. Had they ambushed Sam's guys? Or was Sam right and one of them had been shooting at something that scared him?

Sam shoved the money in the messenger bag and tossed it at Al-Fayed. He caught it easily. Then he spoke to his companion in Arabic—or what she thought was Arabic. She wasn't precisely certain. The other man nodded and said something in return. His fingers were on the detonator. She didn't know if that meant he was ready to blow them up or if he was preventing them from blowing up by the pressure of his fingers.

Her heart slammed her ribs. Was this it? Could it all come down to these next few moments? What if Sam never knew how she felt? Or maybe he did know. How could he not after everything that had happened between them?

"Sam," she choked out.

"Hush, Georgie. I've got this," he said quietly. Soothingly.

Al-Fayed shot them a triumphant look as he retreated to where his gun lay by the door. He picked it up and shoved in the magazine. Coffee Shop Man stood where Al-Fayed had left him, watching the two of them with narrowed eyes.

"You know, maybe I should let him blow you up anyway. You've caused me a lot of trouble," Al-Fayed said as he turned back to them. He lifted his weapon. "Or maybe I should shoot you both and leave you to rot."

She could feel Sam's body tightening as if he were about to spring into action. She didn't know what he planned to do, but she felt like it would be bad for them all if he did anything.

Al-Fayed's barrel swung in her direction all of a sudden. "Move a muscle, John Wayne, and I will kill her. I don't think you'd like that, would you? Now put the gun down or I *will* shoot."

Sam dropped his gun to his side. Al-Fayed laughed. "So you can be reasonable. Eject the magazine and put it on the table."

Sam growled but he did what the man ordered.

"Now Dr. Hayes, if you do not wish your latest boyfriend to die, you will come to me."

Georgie swallowed. "Georgie," Sam said. "Don't."

"I have to." She walked around the table on shaky legs and crossed the room slowly, her heart in her throat the whole way.

When she was close enough, Al-Fayed grabbed her, wrapping an arm around her chest and tugging her against his body. She could feel the sweat beneath his clothes, the tension in his body. He wasn't as calm as he was pretending to be. He said something to Coffee Shop Man in Arabic, and then he dragged her backward, through the door and into the mugginess of the night.

The last thing she saw was Sam's face. It was filled with fear and determination and some other emotion she couldn't quite understand. She should have told him she loved him. Should have said the words and to hell with this evil man dragging her down the steps.

Despair filled her. And anger, because dammit, she wasn't ready to die. Wasn't ready to give up on all the things that had passed between her and Sam. She loved him and she was going to fight for him.

And it began right now. Georgeanne Hayes wasn't giving up. She was made of stronger stuff than that—and it was time she did something to take back her life and her destiny.

―――

AL-FAYED DRAGGED Georgie through the door and Sam's gut churned. He wanted to go after her, but Imran Nassif was standing across the table, calmly holding a bomb's detonator, grinning like a madman. He strode toward the table where he'd left his weapon, let go of the detonator, and shoved the magazine back inside the pistol.

He'd disarmed the bomb at some point, which meant now was Sam's chance. But if he shot this guy, then Al-Fayed might harm Georgie. Sam had to trust that his team was going to rescue her. It was so damned hard not to grab his pistol and end this asshole, but he pulled in deep breaths and didn't move a muscle.

As soon as Nassif was out the door, however, Sam sprang into action, shoving the magazine home and heading for the back door. He couldn't go through the front in case they were waiting for him. Hell, they might be watching the back too. He flicked off all the lights as he went so that he could slip out the door without being spotlighted for whomever might be there.

"Al-Fayed has Georgie," Sam said, knowing his team would hear.

"Hawk's got a bead on him," Richie responded.

Sam's stomach flipped. He knew that the sniper was supposed to be the best in HOT, but if he was off even a millimeter, he could kill Georgie instead of Al-Fayed. "Nassif is wearing a suicide vest."

"We gathered that from the conversation."

"He disarmed it when he retrieved his pistol."

"Flash, you close enough to intercept him?" Richie asked.

"That's an affirmative," Flash responded.

"Then take him down. Alive if possible. And don't get blown up."

"Copy that."

"I'm coming out the backdoor," Sam said. "Where's Georgie now?"

"Christ!" someone hissed. "She's doing something. I can't get a clear shot."

A second later, Sam heard gunfire. Fear skated down his spine, chilling him to the bone. He bolted around the house, uncertain what he might find but determined to save the woman he loved—his Georgie—from any harm. He'd said he'd die if he had to—and he would. Without hesitation if it meant Georgeanne Hayes was alive in this world.

Sam didn't have the benefit of night vision goggles since he'd been operating inside the house, but his team did. He had to trust that was enough. His vision was still adjusting to the dark, but what he saw in front of the house froze his blood.

Georgie was wrapped around Abdullah al-Fayed, screaming bloody murder. Her hands were on his wrist—the one holding the weapon—and she was wrestling for control.

Al-Fayed wasn't much bigger than she was, but he was stronger. Something flashed in his free hand and then he wrenched his arm free, bringing the gun up and around. Swinging it toward Georgie's head.

Sam didn't hesitate. He sprinted toward Al-Fayed, determined to throw himself between Georgie and the weapon. But he was too far and Al-Fayed wasn't that slow. Any second and the trigger would click, the weapon exploding.

And Georgie would be dead.

Sam shouted. Al-Fayed jerked toward the sound—and then he doubled over, screaming in agony. Had Hawk connected? But if the sniper had shot him, why was Al-Fayed still alive?

Sam tackled the man, sending him sprawling. The gun bounced away, hitting the ground with a thick sound. Sam grabbed Al-Fayed's shoulders and slammed him against the ground again and again.

"Knight Rider! Sam, Jesus," somebody said. Strong hands grabbed him and dragged him off the terrorist who lay sobbing in the dirt. "It's okay, you got him. She's safe."

Sam was on his knees and he looked up to see his team surrounding him, grease-painted faces, NVGs on helmets, rifles slung across chests. "Georgie," he croaked out.

Garrett "Iceman" Spencer, the other FNG who'd arrived at HOT right after he did, stepped through the circle, a smaller figure beside him. "She's right here, dude."

Georgie rushed forward and wrapped her arms around his head, pulling him against her. He came up to her chest when he was on his knees. Not a bad place to be, but he didn't want to be there with everyone watching so he got to his feet and gathered her close.

"I fought back, Sam," she said. "I kicked him in the nuts, too. He screamed like a little girl."

It took Sam a moment to process that. Then he laughed in relief for a second before his grip on her tightened. "He could have killed you. You shouldn't have done it."

"I'm tired of other people trying to run my life. I wasn't going to let him make decisions for me. And I'm not letting you either. Just so you know."

"Georgie," he choked out, not trusting himself to say anything else.

"Come on, ladies," Richie said to everyone. "We've got to turn these last two motherfuckers over to the FBI team and clean this place up. Then we have to book it home before Daddy Mendez has a fit."

Sam ran his hands down Georgie's arms, intending to let her go and do his job. Something hot and sticky coated his palm. He pulled it up to the light, his gut twisting at the color. "You're bleeding."

"Am I? I didn't realize... Sam, I feel kinda lightheaded," she said just a second before she went limp in his arms.

Chapter Twenty-One

Georgie was in a hospital bed. That was the first thing she realized when she woke. The second was that she wasn't alone. Sam sat in a chair by the bed, engrossed in his phone. She took a long moment to study him, casting her mind back over the events of the past few days.

He was so handsome, so lonely. Her Sam. Always determined to do the right thing. Determined to sacrifice himself for her. He was still wearing the clothing he'd had on when Al-Fayed and his friend entered the cottage, so she didn't think she'd been in the hospital all that long.

"Sam?"

His head jerked up, his eyes intent on hers. Filled with emotions she couldn't quite pinpoint.

"Hey, G. How you feeling?"

Her arm was sore. It was also bandaged and her head was a little stuffy from whatever pain medication they'd given her. But she was happy. "Great. You're here."

He smiled as he reached for her hand. Their fingers tangled. "I'm glad. You scared me."

"What happened? I don't remember."

"Which part? The part where you attacked a terrorist or what happened afterward?"

"I remember right up until you were holding me when it was over."

He let out a breath. "Then you remember just about everything. We found a knife on the ground. Al-Fayed slashed your arm with it. He was probably trying to stab you, but he missed in the struggle for the gun."

Georgie blinked. "I didn't know. I remember that something stung, but then everything happened so fast I forgot about it."

"Until you lost enough blood to make you dizzy."

"Did I lose that much?"

"Not a lot, but it affects everyone differently. It was probably a combination of blood loss and the adrenaline drop. Iceman's still kicking himself for not checking you over before he brought you to me."

"He didn't have a choice. I was already trying to get to you. He just opened the circle and let me in."

"You're going to be fine, Georgie. The doc stitched you up. There'll be a scar on your upper arm, but the cut was clean and it won't show too bad once it heals."

"Did you call my family?" Her stomach twisted at the thought.

He shook his head and relief flooded her. "I wanted

to, but I figured it was your call. If you'd been hurt worse, I would have called Rick though."

"I'm glad you didn't." She blinked up at the ceiling as relief swamped her. "How long have I been here? And where's Belle?"

"Belle is fine. Evie has her."

"Who's Evie?"

"Matt Girard's fiancée. She'll take good care of Belle until you can get her. As for how long you've been here, you've been asleep a few hours now. Once we realized you were hurt, Ice gave you pain meds. You'd already passed out by then, but they seem to have kept you knocked out."

"Yeah, I'm a bit of a lightweight with pain medication. I don't take anything stronger than Tylenol or I'll be out for hours." It was still dark outside the windows, so at least she hadn't slept until the next day. "What time is it?"

"About two in the morning."

"Oh. Wow. Did you get those guys, Sam?"

He squeezed her hand. "We did. They won't be a problem again."

Georgie bit her lip. "What's going to happen to them?"

"Not sure. And even if I was, I couldn't tell you. But they won't bother you ever again. That much I'm certain of."

She thought of that moment back in the cottage when Al-Fayed had aimed his pistol at Sam. "I'm sorry, Sam, but I had to go with him when he threatened to shoot you. I couldn't let it happen."

He bent and kissed the back of her hand. "I know. You scared the hell out of me, though."

"I wasn't sure the other guy wouldn't blow you both up after we left, but I had to eliminate at least one threat to you."

"I appreciate that, honey. Even if you shaved a few years off my life. The asshole was wearing a dummy bomb, by the way. He had no intention of blowing himself up."

Georgie processed that. "It was a fake? Holy cow."

"Yeah, and I wish I'd known that at the time because I'd have shot them both."

She was kind of glad he hadn't just because she wouldn't have wanted to see that. She didn't imagine it was the kind of thing she'd easily forget. "When can I go home?"

"Probably in the morning once the doctor checks you out again."

She wanted to go home now and snuggle up in bed with Sam, but she'd have to be patient. She thought about what she hadn't said to him before Abdullah Al-Fayed dragged her outside, but now that she had the time and space to tell him how she felt, her throat tightened and the words wouldn't come out. What would happen if she said those words and he didn't return them? Or, worse, he looked at her with pity? Poor little Georgie Hayes with her crush on Sam McKnight.

She couldn't take it if he did that, so she said nothing. Inside, she was a ball of nerves though.

"Georgie, I—" His phone buzzed and he dragged it from his pocket, frowning at whatever he saw there.

For a moment she thought it might be Rick, but her brother wouldn't be calling at two in the morning.

"McKnight," he said. "Yes. Now? I'll be there in ten." He shoved the phone into his pocket and stood. "I'm sorry, G, but I have to go."

Her heart throbbed. "Will you be back?"

"It might be a bit, but I'll be back as soon as I can." He bent and kissed her on the forehead. "You scared me, Georgie. I'm glad you're okay."

Just glad? She swallowed. "I'm glad too."

"I already put Evie's number into your phone, so you can reach her about Belle."

Georgie grabbed his sleeve. "Wait, what? That sounds like you're not coming back at all."

"I am, but I don't know when." He kissed her lips and she opened to him, love and fear flooding her in nearly equal measure. "Be good, G. I'll see you as soon as I can."

Sam strode out the door before she could disentangle the words clogging her throat. Tears pricked her eyes as his footsteps echoed down the hallway, carrying him away from her.

"I love you," she whispered to the empty room.

YOU DIDN'T TELL *her you love her.*

Sam slammed his truck door and shoved the key into the ignition. He'd wanted to tell her, intended to tell her, but then the phone call came and he'd been ordered back to HOT HQ. They'd only just wrapped up the operation with the terrorists who'd killed Jake Hamilton and they were already being sent on another mission.

He didn't know what it was about or where they were going, but he'd known that he couldn't tell Georgie what was in his heart and then walk out on her like that.

Maybe it was a sign that he wasn't supposed to. He'd never intended to fall for her, and he certainly hadn't intended to drag her into this kind of life. He'd lost his head a bit after Al-Fayed took her. He'd been so damned happy she was alive he'd have told her anything she wanted to hear.

But he had his head on straight now. Georgie Hayes wasn't meant for the kind of rough and tumble existence a professional soldier led. Hell, she'd almost lost her life because she'd gotten too close to a Pentagon employee. And Sam's life was way worse than some random sergeant's in the Pentagon.

No, he wasn't ever putting her in that kind of peril again. Best if he drove away and didn't come back. Georgie would move on with her life if he weren't in it. He'd been a diversion for a while, a teenage fantasy that she'd finally gotten to explore. She was a grown woman now and she could do far better than either him or Tim Cash.

Maybe he'd given her back her confidence after Tim had wrecked it. She could find another man, certain she was desirable now.

Sam clenched the wheel like his life depended on it. He didn't want to think of Georgie with another man. It'd nearly killed him when she'd married Tim, and that's when he was still denying how he felt. Now?

Jesus.

Sam stepped on the gas and flew toward HQ. He needed to lose himself in work for awhile. Get his priorities straight again.

Remember that Georgie wasn't ever going to be his.

GEORGIE WAS DISCHARGED the next morning from the private hospital where she'd been treated. She'd never heard of it before but it was called Riverstone. She'd been treated like a VIP and had no complaints. They didn't even ask her for her insurance information, which she found odd, but the discharge nurse told her everything was taken care of and not to worry.

She'd hoped that Sam would be the one to take her home once she was free, but it was someone else who arrived. A soldier in uniform, and not one she'd ever met before. He took her to the military building where Sam had taken her before and deposited her in a plush waiting room.

It wasn't Sam who came through the doors to greet her, though. It was Colonel Mendez. He was smiling as he came over and politely shook her hand. Then he took a seat across from her, his big form seeming to dwarf the chair in which he sat. He was a handsome man, probably somewhere around fifty, and more than a little bit intimidating.

"Thank you for your help, Dr. Hayes. Without you, those men would still be plotting a terror attack on the United States."

Georgie dropped her gaze. "I don't feel like I did much. But I'm glad it was useful." She looked at him again. "Will they be charged for killing Sergeant Hamilton?"

"I think so, yes. Abdullah Al-Fayed confessed when you and Sergeant McKnight were with him last night. We have the conversation recorded. Good work, by the way."

Georgie twisted her fingers together in her lap. She didn't know why she was here, and she didn't know where Sam was. Would he walk in soon?

"You understand that you can't talk with anyone about what happened over the past few days, right?" The colonel looked serious, his dark eyes spearing into her, searching for something.

"I know that, Colonel. I've been teaching military students for more than a year now, and I've had a Pentagon pass for nearly that long. I understand that some things are meant to be kept quiet for national security reasons."

He nodded, seemingly pleased. "Yes, that's correct. It's for your safety, too. The less that's said about your involvement last night, the better."

"Believe me, I don't want to tell anyone. I don't want to be scared all the time and looking over my shoulder."

"You won't have to. We captured the entire cell. They're finished here. The main cell back in their home country has other priorities to chase. They won't be looking for you."

"How can you be sure?"

His eyes flashed even as he smiled a big, wolfish

smile. "I'm sure. They have other fish to fry. Your home is safe, Dr. Hayes. I've sent a team to secure it and install an alarm system as well as cameras. They'll show you how to work everything when you arrive."

"I... Thank you. Could I speak to Sam now?" she added.

He shook his head. "I'm sorry, but his team is downrange. They won't be home for at least a couple of weeks. Maybe more."

Georgie's heart fell. Sam had left. And without saying goodbye. Without saying *anything*. Had he known last night when he got that phone call?

Of course he had. And he'd said nothing.

What had been earth shattering to her was nothing more than sex to him. But he'd told her that, hadn't he? She just hadn't listened.

"If you're ready to go home, Evie is waiting in another room for you. She has your cat."

"Yes," Georgie said, her voice feeling rusty and tight. "I'm ready."

Chapter Twenty-Two

"What the hell happened, Georgie? First there was a guy and now there's no guy." Rick sounded exasperated with her. And more than a little worried.

Georgie sighed and shoved her hair back from her face. "I made him up so you'd stop bothering me."

Of course it wasn't true, but she wasn't telling her brother about Sam. Or about the blissful few days she'd spent wrapped in his arms in a cottage in Maryland.

Her heart ached every time she thought of Sam. She hadn't seen him or heard from him in three weeks. He hadn't been kidding when he'd said his life was unpredictable.

She'd made friends with Evie Baker, who'd told her so much about what life with a Special Operator was like. Evie was gorgeous, a tall black-haired beauty who cooked mouthwatering meals and somehow managed to stay thin.

Georgie had eaten her share of that food over the past three weeks. She'd gone to Evie and Matt's place, and Evie had come over to her kitchen to cook as well. Georgie had even learned a thing or two about how to make simple dishes that were amazingly delicious.

She'd hoped she might get to fix them for Sam, but she wasn't sure that would ever happen. She couldn't get over the fact he hadn't said anything to her about leaving, or when he might be back.

And since she knew how Sam was about anything to do with her, she figured that he wasn't in any hurry to see her again. He'd probably convinced himself that she was too good for him and it was better this way.

Which made her want to knock him over the head with a frying pan.

Rick sighed. "Mother worries about you. I'm just trying to make sure you're all right since she won't ask you herself."

"She won't ask because she knows I'm a grown woman and I can take care of myself." Georgie tapped her pencil against the desk in her home office. "Rick, honestly, I'm happy with what I'm doing. I love my house, I love my job, and I'm not ready to jump into a relationship with anyone." Anyone except Sam. "And while we're at it, I don't appreciate you asking Sam to check on me. He has an important job and he doesn't have time to chase me down just because you ask him to."

"You're right," Rick said on another sigh. "I shouldn't have asked him. I tried calling him recently, but he must be out of the country again."

"He said something about going on a mission. I don't know where."

"How'd he look? Did he seem all right?" She could hear the concern in her brother's voice and it softened her attitude a bit. Rick was a worrier by nature. When he loved someone, he was always concerned about how they were feeling. It was sweet, especially considering how tough her brother was in other ways.

"He seemed fine. It was good to see him."

"You still got a crush on him?" She could hear the laughter in his voice, but it was no laughing matter to her.

"And what if I did? Would you freak if I went out with him?"

She could almost see Rick's face. He'd be blinking right about now. Processing what she'd said. "It would be a little weird for me, sure. He's my best friend and you're my sister. But I suppose I'd get used to it. Why? Is there something you aren't telling me?"

"Not at all. I just like yanking your chain." Because some things were private. Not only that, but her brief affair with Sam McKnight seemed to be over and done at this point. There was nothing to tell.

They talked for a few more minutes—about Hopeful, about their mother's upcoming garden party, about their father's golf trip, about Rick's wife and kids—and then hung up with a promise to speak again soon.

Georgie stared at the phone and heaved a sigh. Talking to Rick, hearing the laughter of his kids in the background, talking about their parents—everything about it made her feel her loneliness keenly. Some days she thought returning to Hopeful was a good idea.

But she usually came to her senses before she put the house on the market and started to pack.

Georgie worked on the syllabus for her next class, which started on Monday, and then decided it was time for bed. She went up to her room, got undressed, and climbed under the covers with her book. Belle jumped on the bed and proceeded to take a bath.

"We lead an exciting life these days, don't we, Belle?"

Belle didn't answer, and Georgie gave up on her book and turned on the news. She must have dozed off because the ringing of her phone scared the hell out of her when it jerked her from sleep. She grabbed it from the bedside table. When Sam's name popped up on the screen, she nearly dropped the phone as she tried to slide the bar before it went to voice mail.

"Hello?"

There was silence on the other end and her heart fell. Dammit, she'd missed him. Would he leave a message? Or would he disappear again and leave her kicking herself for not answering quickly enough?

"Hey there, G."

He sounded so good. Her shoulders sagged with relief—both that she'd caught the call in time and that he obviously wasn't dead. Evie hadn't said much about that bit, but Georgie knew her friend worried about her fiancé every time he went on a mission. Matt wasn't supposed to be deploying as much as he once had, according to Evie, but any deployment was frightening.

"Hey, Sam. Long time, no hear." *Be cool, Georgie.*

He chuckled softly. "Yeah. I told you that could happen, didn't I?"

"You did. I just didn't realize you meant quite so literally or quickly."

"That's what life with me is like, babe. Here one day, gone the next. Radio silence for weeks. I tried to tell you."

"I know, and I appreciate it."

"Still think it's something you can handle?"

Georgie's heart sped up just a little. Was he saying what she thought he was saying? Or was he just making conversation. "I could learn to handle it."

"Are you sure about that? Because it won't be easy, G."

She swallowed as tears welled behind her eyes. He wouldn't be asking if he wasn't leaning in her direction. "I know. But you're worth it, Sam. You're worth it to me."

He didn't say anything and she strained to hear him, wondering if he'd hung up on her.

"You still there?"

"Yeah, I'm here."

She let out a shaky sigh. "So where are you now? Back in the CONUS?" She loved that she could use military lingo with him and know, at least a little bit, what she was talking about. She'd already known a lot, but Evie had taught her even more.

She thought he might be grinning. "I am."

"Which part of the CONUS?"

This time he laughed. "You like saying that, don't you?"

She smiled. "Who wouldn't? The military has such interesting terms for things, don't you think? CONUS for continental US. TDY. AWOL. Hoo-ah. It's fascinating."

"I didn't call you for a lesson on military acronyms, babe."

"No, I don't suppose you did." Her heart was filling with warmth as they talked. "So where are you right now?"

"Right now?"

"Right damn now."

"Standing on your front steps. Wondering if I should ring the bell or go."

Georgie gasped. And then she dropped the phone in her haste to get out of bed. "Don't you dare leave, Sam!" she yelled as she grappled for the phone in her covers.

She ran down the stairs and yanked open the front door after punching in the alarm code. Sam stood there with his phone to his ear. He lowered his arm slowly. They stared at each other.

"Looking kinda sexy in my shirt, G," he said softly.

She crossed her arms self-consciously. She was wearing one of his T-shirts that she'd swiped at the cottage. It was not sexy. It swam on her. But it made her think of him, and so she wore it anyway even though she got hot in the middle of the night and had to sleep on top of the covers.

"I missed you," she said simply, her eyes welling with tears. "So much."

"I missed you too." He cocked his head to the side. "You still naked down there?"

"I'm wearing panties."

His teeth flashed white in the darkness. "I meant something else. Thought about that a lot out in the field this time. Damned embarrassing a couple of times, if you know what I mean."

"The fellas don't appreciate a good hard-on?" she teased, her heart racing a mile a minute.

"Oh, I think we all appreciate them. When they belong to us and there's a hot woman to appreciate it with us in private."

"I see."

He came the rest of the way up the steps until he loomed over her. He was wearing desert-camouflage and he looked utterly delicious. Her every fantasy come to life.

"Gonna invite me in?"

"That depends."

He looked suddenly wary. "On what?"

Georgie held the door tightly, like she needed it to stand. Or maybe to keep from flinging herself in his arms before she had an answer. "On why you're here. Is it for a hot fuck? Or something else?"

———

SAM LOOKED at her standing there in his T-shirt, her pretty green eyes fixed on his face, all the hurt and confusion she felt showing in them, and he wanted to drag her in his arms and just hold her tight.

Why was he here? Because he loved her and he couldn't stop thinking about her. Because he'd left the hospital determined to make a clean break with her, for her sake, and then he'd been haunted by memories of her on the mission. Oh, not when it counted. When it counted, he was able to blank his mind of everything but the job.

But when he wasn't busting his ass crossing through a hot desert or bursting into a compound to rescue frightened tourists who'd been taken hostage by yet another group with an axe to grind against Americans, he'd thought of Georgie and the way she made him feel.

Like he belonged. Like he was special. Like he'd come home.

But the words he wanted to say lodged in his throat. He was afraid of rejection after all this time. After everything that had passed between them. What if Georgie only wanted him for a hot fuck? It was possible. She'd said as much in the cottage.

Finally, he managed to speak. He hoped it was good enough.

"I'm here because I need you. Because I missed you. Because, when I thought of everything I wanted to do when I got back, none of it meant a damn thing if you weren't a part of it."

She wrapped a hand in his shirt and tugged him toward her. He entered the house, waited for her to shut the door and lock it. And then he pushed her back against the door and buried his face in her hair.

"Georgeanne. God, I missed you." She smelled so

sweet, like flowers and cake, and he wanted to devour her.

Her arms looped around his neck. She splayed a hand over the back of his head. "Sam. Oh, Sam. Don't you leave me like that again."

There was a lump in his throat. "I already told you—"

"I know. You have to go when you have to go. But you don't have to go without telling me you want me again. You don't have to let me think you're finished with me. With us. Maybe I can handle you leaving if I know you still need me."

He nuzzled the side of her neck. "I'm not sure I'll ever be finished."

She squeezed him tight then. Her body trembled. "I love you, Sam. I don't care if that makes you uncomfortable. I love you and I won't keep it a secret any longer. From anyone."

His heart had stopped beating in his chest. And then it lurched forward again, beating harder and faster than before. He straightened so he could see her eyes.

She bit her lip, that sweet plump lip that he wanted to nibble and suck. "I'm sorry if that bothers you. But I can't help it and I won't hide it. And if that makes you want to run away, then I guess I'll have to fight to keep you from doing it."

His throat ached. "Run away? No fucking chance. It makes me want to strip you naked and worship every inch of your body until I can't move anymore."

She feathered her fingers over his cheek. They were trembling. "You'll have to be a little plainer with me,

Sam. Tell me what it means that you aren't running. Tell me what this is to you. What *I* am to you."

His heart hammered. "I can't forget you, Georgie. I can't quit you either. I've thought of you for twelve years —longer—and once I had you—really had you—I knew I was in trouble. Because I don't care how pissed off Rick gets at me, or how disappointed your parents are because I'm not what they envisioned for their princess. I want you. I need you." He swallowed the rock in his throat. Jesus, was he going to frigging pass out here? Why were the words so damn difficult to say? "You're everything to me," he finished, disappointed in himself for not being able to say the three words he wanted to say.

The words that terrified him because they were so big and important. So life-altering.

He'd tried like hell to dig her out of his heart, but he couldn't do it. She was the one obstacle he couldn't defeat.

No, not an obstacle. The best damn thing to ever happen to him.

She smiled in spite of his lack of finesse with words. "You love me. I knew it." She gave him a smug look. "Bet you fell for me when I was following you around the house all those years ago. God knows I was pretty irresistible."

He laughed and ached all at once. "About as irresistible as a rash."

She pinched his arm and he laughed again. "You're a hot mess, Sam."

"You make me crazy, Georgeanne." He ran his

hands up her sides, under the T-shirt, and cupped her warm breasts in his palms.

"You make me crazy too. And I don't know how this is going to work out, and I can't guarantee I won't freak out when you're gone, but I love you and I want to try. I'm tired of playing it safe. If it doesn't work, then at least we'll know. But I want that chance. I need that chance."

He ran his thumbs over her nipples, thrilled to hear the catch of her breath. "I know. I need that chance too. I need you. And it's gonna work, babe. I know it. There's nobody else for me."

"Me neither. Not since I realized what boys were all about and you were there with Rick all the time, looking so sexy and unattainable."

He grinned. "That long?"

She nodded emphatically. "That damn long."

He dipped his head and kissed her lightly, though she tried to deepen the kiss. He pulled back while she whimpered, shaping her breasts with his palms. "I've thought of little else but this for the last three weeks."

"You know what I thought about?"

He shook his head. She unbuckled his belt, unbuttoned his pants—and then her hands wrapped around his swollen cock. He didn't know what to expect—but she dropped to her knees and tilted her head back to look up at him.

"This," she said. "I thought about this."

And then she took him in her mouth and his knees nearly buckled.

"God. Georgie." He braced a hand against the wall

and swallowed. Her tongue rolled over him, her fingers pumped him, and it would just be so frigging easy to let her get him off this way.

But it wasn't what he'd envisioned during the long, lonely stretches on watch. He reached for her, pulled her up and ripped the shirt she wore over her head at the same time. Then he filled his hands and mouth with her breasts. She clutched his shoulders, gasping, and he knew what an utterly perfect night he was in for.

But he suddenly didn't want it here, like this, in her hallway. Up against a wall. There was plenty of time for that kind of thing, but right now he wanted her beneath him in a bed. Wanted her legs around him and her mouth on his.

He swept an arm behind her legs and scooped her into his arms. And then he took the stairs two at a time. When he reached her room, the television was on and the cat was parked in the middle of the bed.

Belle took one look at the two of them and bolted. Sam laid Georgie on the bed and stripped her panties off. Then he was between her legs, his pants shoved down his hips, rolling on a condom with shaking hands.

And then finally, finally, he was inside her. Loving her. Feeling the utter rightness of what she did to him. He loved her cries, loved her breathy moans. She shattered quickly, her body tightening around his, her inner muscles squeezing him hard, his name on her lips.

He followed her over the edge, a groan ripping from his throat. And then he held her, his heart beating hard, and knew he'd only ever felt this way with her. This exhilarating rush of emotions and sensations.

Sam propped himself on an elbow, pushed the hair off Georgie's face, and smiled down at her. "I love you," he whispered, finally finding his voice for what he wanted to say. "I love you so much."

Her eyes glistened and she smiled that beautiful smile that he felt belonged to him alone.

"I know," she said. "And you have no idea how happy that makes me."

Warmth blossomed inside him. This felt so right. Here, with Georgie. His tormenter. His love. "I'll do the best I can to make you happy. Always."

"I know you will. I believe in you."

Her faith in him was a gift beyond measure. "You have no idea what it does to me to hear you say that."

She traced her fingers over his lips, softly, lightly. "You're mine now, Sam. I'm not letting you go. Ever."

"There's no one else I'd rather belong to." He tucked his head into her shoulder and breathed her in as belonging filled his soul. "*You* are my home, Georgie. Only you. Always you."

She punched him lightly on the arm. "Damn you," she whispered and he looked up to see tears sliding down her cheeks. "I didn't want to cry."

He grinned at her. "Who's the hot mess now, huh?"

"I blame you." She swiped the tears away and pushed at him until he rolled over. He was still half in and half out of his camos. Her fingers went to the buttons of his shirt, flicking them free.

"You'll have to pay for making me cry," she said as she opened his shirt and pushed up the T-shirt beneath. Then she sat up and stared at him before slowly shaking her head. "Wow, who knew a uniform, tattoos, and muscles could be so appealing?"

She picked up his dog tags where they lay against his skin, fingering the edges. Then she dropped them again and stretched out on top of him.

"What happened to making me pay?" he asked when she just lay there and hugged him.

"I'll get to that," she murmured against his skin. "Right now, I want this. Just you and me and our hearts beating together."

He slid his arms around her and squeezed. "That's what I want too. Forever."

Epilogue

Texas in the fall was still hotter than blazes. But Sam McKnight was even hotter. Georgie watched him laugh at something her father said, watched as his long, tanned fingers gripped the beer bottle he'd set down earlier and lifted it to his lips.

She watched the slide of his throat, thought of how she owned that throat. Of how she owned those muscles, every last one, and how lucky she was and how jealous every other girl at her mother's garden party had to be.

Well, except maybe the married ones.

Georgie's gaze glided over toward Sue Sugarton, who kept throwing glances toward Sam. Don Sugarton was currently stuffing his second hamburger in his face, oblivious.

All right, maybe the married ones too then.

"I swear, Georgie, if you keep looking at that man like that, I'm going to have a lot of explaining to do at the next Junior League meeting."

Georgie grinned at her mother. Cynthia Tolliver Hayes looked perfectly gorgeous in a pink linen summer dress and cream kitten heels. She also did not look as disapproving as she sounded. Quite the opposite, in fact, if her serene smile was any indication.

"I can't help it," Georgie said. "I'm in love."

Her mother took a sip of her virgin pink cocktail. "He is too. And it's wonderful to see."

Georgie frowned. "He was afraid you wouldn't approve. I had a hell of a time getting him down here."

"Not approve? We love Sam!"

"I know that." She gazed over at him again. "Maybe he knows it now too. Dad's being awfully great about the whole thing."

"Your father is a fabulous judge of character. He's never suffered one moment of doubt over Sam McKnight. Tim, on the other hand…"

"I know." Georgie sighed. If she'd listened to her father in the first place, maybe she wouldn't have married Tim. Not that he'd tried to talk her out of it, but he had certainly never cared for Tim much. That should have been her first clue.

"Rick's having a little trouble adjusting," her mother said, and Georgie's gaze strayed to where her brother sat with his wife. "But he'll get used to it."

Rick hadn't taken the news badly, but he hadn't been precisely joyful either. In fact, he'd taken Sam aside for what she could only surmise was a man-to-man talk. He'd looked stern, but then so had Sam, and she'd known Sam was fighting for her.

And that was a long cry from where he'd been just a

few weeks ago when he'd been willing to walk away because of his fears over what her family would think.

"I know. I guess I can't blame him. Sam was his best friend in the world, and I've sort of stolen him away. He's my best friend now."

"Your brother will adjust, dear. Oh my, Lilly Beth is about to cause a mischief and her parents aren't even looking. Excuse me."

Georgie watched her mother hurry away and then her gaze strayed back to Sam. He was looking straight at her this time, and she felt that familiar wash of heat she always felt when he was near. He said something to her dad and then he was moving her way.

"How you doing?" she asked when he reached her side.

He sat in the chair beside her and took a sip of his beer. "It's a little awkward, but it's fine."

She turned her head, met his dark gaze. "You aren't just saying that?"

"No. Because you're worth it to me, Georgie. Some things in this life are worth fighting for, and you're one of them."

"That's mighty sweet of you to say."

"It's not sweet when it's the truth. When you were in danger, all I wanted to do was fight for you. I'd have killed those men for daring to frighten you if I could have."

She put her palm on his cheek, watched his eyes darken. "I'm glad you're here with me. I'm glad you decided to keep fighting. Because I love you. I always have. And I always will."

"You sure about that? Always is a mighty long time."

"I'm aware of it. And yes, I'm sure."

He grinned. "Speaking of a long time, you think we've been here long enough? I want to show you some things back at the hotel."

She leaned in and kissed him. "What kind of things, handsome?"

"Dirty things, G. Hot, messy things. Things that will make your toes curl."

"Oh, I am *so* in."

"I hoped you'd say that." They stood and he took her hand, but he didn't move for a long moment. "Damn, I love you."

Happiness flooded her. "Of course you do. I'm awesome."

He grinned. "Humble too."

She squeezed his hand. "Mostly, I'm happy. You make me that way."

"Then you're really going to love what comes next, babe."

She had no doubt. Whether it was Sam McKnight in her bed or just giving her a hot look from across a room, she was going to love every damn moment of being with him. Because that's the way it was always meant to be.

"So long as it involves you and me somewhere alone, I know I will."

They started across the yard. But Sam suddenly stopped and she turned toward him in confusion. He was watching her with a serious expression on his face.

"I know this isn't the time to ask, so I'm not asking,

but what do you think about getting married someday? I know your last marriage wasn't so hot—"

He didn't get a chance to finish the sentence because she flung her arms around him and kissed him. He caught her to him and held her tight. When they came up for air again, somebody whistled.

"Yes," she said. "The minute you ask me, the answer is yes."

"Damn, I wish I had a ring so I could do it now."

"You don't need a ring."

He frowned. And then he reached beneath his shirt and pulled out his dog tags. When he dropped to one knee, Georgie gasped. So did everyone else.

"Will you marry me, Georgeanne Hayes? I know I'm not a rich man, but if love were currency, I'd have a fortune. And it'd all be yours. It already is."

Georgie sniffled as she took the dog tags he offered her. She'd imagined Sam asking her to marry him a million times when she was a teenager. She'd even imagined it recently. But not one time was a perfect as this one. Because this was the real one, and it was so Sam.

"Yes, I'll marry you, Sam McKnight. You have my heart. You always have. And I know you'll protect it for the rest of our lives."

He stood and dragged her into his arms. "Damn straight I will," he growled.

"Let's get out of here. I want to celebrate this moment alone."

He glanced over her head. "I do too, but I think we've got to stay a little longer now. Your mother's crying. Your dad is patting her and giving me a thumbs up. I think we need to let them enjoy this moment with us. At least for a little while."

Georgie squeezed him tight. He was right, even if she didn't want to share him with anyone just now. "Okay, but as soon as we get back to the hotel, I want you naked."

Sam grinned. "No problem, babe."

He kissed her again and then he set her away from him and took her hand. Her family swarmed around them, laughing and hugging and proclaiming their happiness. Even Rick.

It was the perfect way to celebrate their future. Right here with the family she loved. The family who'd always loved Sam and always would. Just like she did.

STRIKE TEAM 1 gathered at Richie and Evie's place fairly often. Evie was an amazing cook, and they all liked to eat. Kev shoveled a forkful of delicious Cajun food into his mouth and thanked the good Lord that he'd burn it all off in training tomorrow. The sauce was rich, the rice beneath it fluffy and filling.

Richie leaned over and kissed Evie. "Damn, *cher*. You've done it again."

Evie smiled. "Cooking delicious meals is part of my dastardly plan to keep you forever."

"It's working," Richie said.

"You can keep me," Flash added as he tore off a hunk of French bread.

"Nope," Richie said. "You aren't house-trained yet."

Kid snorted. The rest of the guys chuckled. Knight Rider sat beside his fiancée and looked about as happy as a man could look. They kept bumping shoulders and sharing looks. Hell, they'd only been engaged for about a month at this point but they looked like they couldn't wait to get married. Knight Rider had said they weren't in a rush. Apparently, there was a wedding being planned in Texas next year. Like Richie, Georgie came from money—and her family was planning to do it up big.

Richie and Evie were getting married too, but they hadn't set a date yet.

Kev concentrated on his food as he thought about the last time he'd gone to a teammate's wedding.

Lucky, looking as beautiful as a bride could look, gliding down the aisle toward Marco. Kev had been the best man and he'd stood there with a giant stone in his gut as he watched the woman he'd always wanted marry his best friend. His fault because he'd walked away from her when she could have been his.

Let Marco have her without a fight—and regretted it every single day from that moment on.

Kev took a swallow of beer, trying to wash away bitter memories. Marco was dead and Lucky wasn't speaking to any of them anymore. She'd left. Moved away and gone silent. She was out of his life for good. So why couldn't he stop thinking about her?

He saw her when he closed his eyes at night. Sometimes, he made love to her in his dreams, though he didn't really know what that would be like. And he always felt like shit when he woke up and realized what he'd been imagining. She'd been Marco's, and he had no right.

"Hey, Big Mac," Hawk said.

Kev jerked. "Yeah?"

"You hear from Lucky lately?"

Kev's gut twisted. He hadn't been expecting that question, but he clearly wasn't the only one remembering the last time a teammate got married. "No."

"Did she really move to Hawaii?"

"That's what I heard," Kev said. Not that Lucky had told him where she was going. The information had been filtered through the HOT grapevine.

"Man, must be nice out there. I guess she deserves it after everything."

"Yeah," Kid added sadly. "I guess she does. If you talk to her, tell her I said hi."

Kev knew that request was aimed at him. Everyone seemed to think that he and Lucky were close since he and Marco had been. They had no idea.

"If I hear from her, I definitely will."

The silence was awkward for a few seconds.

Evie stood up. "Anybody want dessert?"

"Oh hell yes," Iceman said. "What did you make?"

Evie's eyes sparkled. "A bananas Foster cheesecake."

There were moans of delight around the table. "Damn, woman," Richie said. "You trying to fatten up my operators?"

"Oh please. You guys are too active for that. Georgie, can you get the dessert plates while I get the cheesecake?"

"Absolutely," Georgie replied, sliding from her seat to join Evie in the kitchen.

The party finally ended after they'd played poker and drank beer and ate more cheesecake. It was dark out by then, and they said goodbye on the front porch and went to their vehicles.

Kev started his truck and sat there for a long moment, watching as his friends drove away. In spite of the good food and friendship, in spite of how much he loved his team—and Evie and Georgie—there was a hole in his chest that wouldn't quite close. He filled it up, or covered it over, when he was with these people.

But then, when he was alone like now, the hole opened again and he felt empty inside. He didn't know how to fix it, or if he even could. His mind turned to thoughts of Lucky, but he quickly pushed them away.

Lucky wasn't his. She never would be. And he had to forget all about her.

Maybe then the hole inside him would finally close…

―――

If you want to find out what happens when Kev is sent to bring Lucky back to HOT HQ for a mission, be sure to read DANGEROUSLY HOT. It's explosive!

> "Edge of seat action and drama and heart-breaking love all rolled up into a wonderful story." ~ Goodreads

DANGEROUSLY HOT Sneak Peek

December
North Shore, Oahu
Hawaii

Lucky flipped the surfboard upright after she paddled to shore and stepped out onto the sand. It was a typically beautiful Hawaiian day—or it would have been if she hadn't just spotted the man standing cross-armed at the top of the shore break. For a second, she thought her eyes were playing tricks on her. There was no way that Kevin MacDonald was standing up there waiting for her.

But the mirage didn't fade, and her heart reacted with a crazy rhythm that made her head swim. Part of her wanted to turn around and race back out to sea. Part of her wanted to march up to him and plant a fist in his handsome face.

And part of her wanted to wrap her arms around him and hold him tight.

Lucky hardened her heart and lifted her head. She wasn't running, damn him. She thought he'd given up. The phone calls had ceased months ago, and even though it had made her ache deep down, she figured he'd finally gotten the message.

Looks like she'd been wrong.

She clutched the board tighter to her side and climbed the sharply sloping beach at Waimea Bay.

Kev stood impassive, arms crossed, chewing gum like he had no cares in the world, aviator sunglasses reflecting her wet form. Like he belonged here. Like he showed up every day and watched her paddle out to sea before turning and shooting the pipeline back to the beach.

Except he didn't look like he belonged at all. A white T-shirt stretched across his broad chest, tapering down to disappear into the waistband of a pair of faded, loose-fitting Levis. His only real nod to beach culture was a pair of flip-flops, or *slippahs*, as the Hawaiians called them, and she knew it must have given him pause to don them. Kev was usually a cowboy or combat boot kind of guy.

Fresh anger flared to life inside her. But before she could speak, he said the one thing guaranteed to make her listen. Guaranteed to make her wish she were dead.

"Al Ahmad's back."

A cold finger of dread slid deep into her belly, tickled her spine, threatened to turn her knees to liquid. *Al Ahmad.*

He was supposed to be dead. She'd slept at night

because he was dead. Because he could never come for her. Never force her to listen to that lovely, evil voice ever again.

"And what's that mean to me?" she asked. She didn't bother to ask how the bastard was still alive. If Kev was here, then he just was. It wasn't debatable.

But she wasn't about to let Kev know just how horrified that information made her or how much she wanted to sink into the ocean and never come out again.

"We need you, Lucky."

Her breath seized in her lungs. "No way in hell," she said hoarsely when she could talk again. "I'm not on active duty anymore."

As if that had anything to do with it. When she'd been active, she'd wanted to be a part of the Hostile Operations Team. She'd gotten her wish when she'd been assigned to them for interpreter duties. It wasn't the excitement of full-blown ops, but it was important.

She'd been so idealistic. Though women weren't allowed to go on missions, she'd wanted to be the first. She'd hoped she'd get the chance to train hard and save the world, but she'd learned just how unsuited she was for that task, thanks to Al Ahmad.

"We could reactivate you."

Lucky clutched the surfboard harder, the urge to gut him with it burning into her. He stood there so casually, threatening to upend her world as if it were nothing. Threatening to drag her back into that life when it had nearly destroyed her. "Mendez wouldn't dare."

"You know he would."

Lucky slicked back her wet hair with one hand, hoping it didn't shake, and bent to remove the ankle strap anchoring the surfboard to her leg. She didn't have to look at Kev to know he was following the movement of her leg as she thrust it to the side to reach the strap.

She could feel the burn of his gaze on her skin, just like she always had. And it made her sick to her stomach. Angry. How dare he make her feel *anything*.

Especially now.

She hardened her heart. She wouldn't do it. She couldn't do it. She owed them nothing. She'd done her time, and she'd gotten the hell out. She straightened and lifted her chin. "Get someone else. You've got any number of people who can interpret for you."

Those firm lips turned down in a frown. "It's more than translation. We need you on the inside."

Her heart thumped. "I'm not in that business anymore."

As if she ever had been. Her *stay* with Al Ahmad had not been planned. His people had grabbed her at a market in North Africa when she should have been out of their reach. They'd proven she wasn't. That none of them were.

Day after day, she'd thought her life was over. Day after day, he'd toyed with her. Poisoned her mind.

Broke her.

She faced Kev head on, a current of defiance growing inside her with every second. No way in hell was she letting them shatter her carefully reconstructed life. It didn't matter that Al Ahmad had resurfaced, that she damn well wanted to nail the bastard to the wall with a rusty railroad spike.

If she were a different person, a braver person, she would take this chance. She'd get close enough to kill him herself. And then maybe she could forget how weak she was. How needy. How malleable she'd been in his hands. She'd fought him, but not hard enough.

Kev pulled the sunglasses from his face and tapped them against a muscled forearm wrapped in ink. "This is too important. It's you we need. No one else."

Lucky had to remind herself to breathe when faced with the full effect of blue eyes and silky, dark hair that was much longer than Army regs allowed. But Kev was a Spec Ops soldier, and that made the rules different for him.

Women, as she knew from first-hand observation, couldn't help but fling themselves in the path of Kevin MacDonald. Which was precisely why she'd been determined not to do so when they'd first met a couple of years ago. There'd been something between them, some spark, but she'd never found out what it was. Because as quickly as it ignited, it was gone.

It still hurt, remembering the way he'd held her so close when he'd gotten her out of Al Ahmad's compound, the way he'd seemed so intent upon her. He'd kissed her. The one and only time he'd ever done so.

Even now, her lips tingled with the memory. Her body ached with heat.

But it had been nothing more than a beautiful lie.

When she'd looked for him afterward, when she'd expected him to come to the hospital to see her, it had been Marco who came instead.

And now Marco was dead, and she had no right to feel anything but grief. Yet that didn't stop her belly from churning at the sight of Kevin MacDonald.

He watched her with an intensity that both unnerved and angered her. How dare he walk back into her life looking like something straight from a Hollywood movie set and calmly inform her that her world was about to be turned topsy-turvy?

Again.

She picked up the surfboard and started up the beach. "Go tell Mendez to reactivate me," she called over her shoulder. If they wanted her back, they had to force her. "If he could do it, he'd have done it already."

"Aw, sweetheart, don't be like that," Kev said in that Alabama drawl of his, and she stopped short, swung around as fury lashed into her.

"Don't you *dare* call me that!"

He held up both hands, backed away a step. "It's all right, I can take a hint. No sweet nothings." He dropped his hands to his sides, but not before sliding the sunglasses back into place over those beautiful eyes. "But you and I both know Mendez could reactivate you with a phone call. Don't make it happen, Lucky. Help us out, you're done. Get recalled to duty, and God knows what comes next when this is over."

Hell, yes, Mendez could do it. She knew that. But it would take slightly longer than one phone call.

"Tell him I'll think about it," she said, but she

wouldn't do anything of the sort. Yes, she'd love to get Al Ahmad. But she'd like to live even more.

"He's dangerous. You know that better than most." He seemed to hesitate for a second. "Marco would want you to help us get him."

Lucky whipped the surfboard in an arc and let it go. Kev leaped backward as it crashed to the ground. He stumbled and fell against a coconut palm, the fronds shaking with the impact.

"Jesus Christ," he yelled. "What's the matter with you?"

She was shaking. "Don't you *ever* tell me what Marco would want. Invoking his name won't get you anywhere with me."

Kev looked solemn. For the first time since he'd started talking, she felt like she was seeing the real him. The man who'd called her almost nightly for months, trying to make sure she was all right. That Marco's death hadn't killed her too.

"We all lost him, Lucky. We all miss him."

Tears boiled near the surface. Fury ate at her like battery acid. He had no idea. *No idea.*

Of course she missed Marco. And yet she'd been so wrong for him. She'd tried hard to love him the way she should, but loving anyone after what she'd been through with Al Ahmad hadn't been easy.

The guilt of her failures ate at her. She'd been doing a good job of forgetting out here in the sun and surf, of moving on and accepting her life, and Kev was wrecking it all.

"You let him die out there."

It wasn't what she'd meant to say, but she couldn't call the words back now that she'd released them. Kev looked as if she'd slapped him. She knew Marco's death wasn't his fault, but that hadn't stopped her from blaming him—blaming all of Marco's team—for what had happened.

She should apologize, but her throat seized up.

Kev's jaw tightened. "That's not fair, and you know it. Marco died doing the job. It's a risk we all take."

Yes, she knew it. And it was the thing that kept her awake at night sometimes, thinking about Marco, about Kev, wondering if he was still alive or if he'd met his end in some dank, lonely, war-torn country the way Marco had.

But she couldn't say any of that. They stood there staring at each other until Kev took something from his pocket. He held out a card.

"I'm at the Hale Koa. Call me when you've thought about this."

She still couldn't speak. How could she say all the things she needed to say? The things she'd bottled up for so long? How could she ever explain where it had all gone wrong?

He didn't put the card away. She wanted to leave him standing there, but her feet seemed stuck in the sand.

"Take it, Lucky."

She snatched the card from his grasp with a growl. Then she picked up the surfboard and trod up the beach, feeling his eyes on her back the whole way.

HOT Mess

Get DANGEROUSLY HOT at your favorite retailer's website or ask them to order a copy for you to pick up at the store!

Books by Lynn Raye Harris

The Hostile Operations Team ® Books
Strike Team 1

Book 0: RECKLESS HEAT

Book 1: HOT PURSUIT - Matt & Evie

Book 2: HOT MESS - Sam & Georgie

Book 3: DANGEROUSLY HOT - Kev & Lucky

Book 4: HOT PACKAGE - Billy & Olivia

Book 5: HOT SHOT - Jack & Gina

Book 6: HOT REBEL - Nick & Victoria

Book 7: HOT ICE - Garrett & Grace

Book 8: HOT & BOTHERED - Ryan & Emily

Book 9: HOT PROTECTOR - Chase & Sophie

Book 10: HOT ADDICTION - Dex & Annabelle

Book 11: HOT VALOR - Mendez & Kat

Book 12: A HOT CHRISTMAS MIRACLE - Mendez & Kat

The Hostile Operations Team ® Books
Strike Team 2

Book 1: HOT ANGEL - Cade & Brooke

Book 2: HOT SECRETS - Sky & Bliss

Book 3: HOT JUSTICE - Wolf & Haylee

Book 4: HOT STORM - Mal & Scarlett

Book 5: HOT COURAGE ~ Coming Soon!

The HOT SEAL Team Books

Book 1: HOT SEAL - Dane & Ivy

Book 2: HOT SEAL Lover - Remy & Christina

Book 3: HOT SEAL Rescue - Cody & Miranda

Book 4: HOT SEAL BRIDE - Cash & Ella

Book 5: HOT SEAL REDEMPTION - Alex & Bailey

Book 6: HOT SEAL TARGET - Blade & Quinn

Book 7: HOT SEAL HERO - Ryan & Chloe

Book 8: HOT SEAL DEVOTION - Zach & Kayla

Book 9: Shade's book! It's coming. Whether he believes it or not....

HOT Heroes for Hire: Mercenaries
Black's Bandits

Book 1: BLACK LIST - Jace & Maddy

Book 2: BLACK TIE - Brett & Tallie

Book 3: BLACK OUT - Colt & Angie

Book 4: BLACK KNIGHT - Jared & Libby

Book 5: BLACK HEART - Ian Black!

The HOT Novella in Liliana Hart's MacKenzie Family Series

HOT WITNESS - Jake & Eva

---

7 Brides for 7 Brothers

MAX (Book 5) - Max & Ellie

7 Brides for 7 Soldiers

WYATT (Book 4) - Max & Ellie

7 Brides for 7 Blackthornes

ROSS (Book 3) - Ross & Holly

Filthy Rich Billionaires

Book 1: FILTHY RICH REVENGE

Book 2: FILTHY RICH PRINCE

———

Who's HOT?

Strike Team 1

Matt "Richie Rich" Girard (Book 0 & 1)
Sam "Knight Rider" McKnight (Book 2)
Kev "Big Mac" MacDonald (Book 3)
Billy "the Kid" Blake (Book 4)
Jack "Hawk" Hunter (Book 5)
Nick "Brandy" Brandon (Book 6)
Garrett "Iceman" Spencer (Book 7)
Ryan "Flash" Gordon (Book 8)
Chase "Fiddler" Daniels (Book 9)
Dex "Double Dee" Davidson (Book 10)

Commander
John "Viper" Mendez (Book 11 & 12)

Deputy Commander
Alex "Ghost" Bishop

Strike Team 2

Cade "Saint" Rodgers (Book 1)
Sky "Hacker" Kelley (Book 2)
Dean "Wolf" Garner (Book 3)
Malcom "Mal" McCoy (Book 4)
Noah "Easy" Cross
Ryder "Muffin" Hanson
Jax "Gem" Stone
Zane "Zany" Scott
Jake "Harley" Ryan (HOT WITNESS)

SEAL Team 1

Dane "Viking" Erikson (Book 1)
Remy "Cage" Marchand (Book 2)
Cody "Cowboy" McCormick (Book 3)
Cash "Money" McQuaid (Book 4)
Alexei "Camel" Kamarov (Book 5)
Adam "Blade" Garrison (Book 6)
Ryan "Dirty Harry" Callahan (Book 7)
Zach "Neo" Anderson (Book 8)
Corey "Shade" Vance

Black's Bandits

Jace Kaiser (Book 1)
Brett Wheeler (Book 2)
Colton Duchaine (Book 3)
Jared Fraser (Book 4)
Ian Black (Book 5)

Tyler Scott
Thomas "Rascal" Bradley
Dax Freed
Jamie Hayes
Mandy Parker (Airborne Ops)
Melanie (Reception)
? Unnamed Team Members

Freelance Contractors

Lucinda "Lucky" San Ramos, now MacDonald (Book 3)
Victoria "Vee" Royal, now Brandon (Book 6)
Emily Royal, now Gordon (Book 8)
Miranda Lockwood, now McCormick (SEAL Team Book 3)
Bliss Bennett, (Strike Team 2, Book 2)
Angelica "Angie" Turner (Black's Bandits, Book 3)

About the Author

Lynn Raye Harris is a Southern girl, military wife, wannabe cat lady, and horse lover. She's also the New York Times and USA Today bestselling author of the HOSTILE OPERATIONS TEAM ® SERIES of military romances, and 20 books about sexy billionaires for Harlequin.

A former finalist for the Romance Writers of America's Golden Heart Award and the National Readers Choice Award, Lynn lives in Alabama with her handsome former-military husband, one fluffy princess of a cat, and a very spoiled American Saddlebred horse who enjoys bucking at random in order to keep Lynn on her toes.

Lynn's books have been called "exceptional and emotional," "intense," and "sizzling" -- and have sold in excess of 4.5 million copies worldwide.

To connect with Lynn online:
www.LynnRayeHarris.com
Lynn@LynnRayeHarris.com

a BB f g ⓞ

Made in the USA
Middletown, DE
20 September 2023